ALL LIES

The following historical novels are also
by David Macpherson

Defenders of Mai-dun.
A story of the Roman invasion of Dorset

Nomad.
A story of the Tibetan Uprising

A Zigzag Path.
A story of smuggling in the 19th Century

The Black Box
A story of Monmouth's Rebellion
and the Bloody Assizes

Aquarius (pub in 2016)
A story of the building of the Dorchester Aqueduct

All are available through Amazon and Kindle

All Lies

A Story of the Portland Spy Ring

David Macpherson

Prologue

The smoking room of the Athenaeum was a gloomy place even in the gentle light of a summer evening, but the poor illumination permitted anyone who valued his privacy to sit undisturbed. A small group of elderly men in one corner fluttered round Anthony Blunt, soon-to-be knighted for his work as Surveyor of the Queen's pictures, as he pontificated on the undervalued merits of Nicholas Poussin.

In the window alcove a figure almost lost in the half-light sat gazing at the mahogany chessboard in front of him. Sir Roger Hollis, Director of MI5 liked to be undisturbed. The modern replicas of the Lewis chessmen, made from red and white resin rather than walrus ivory, were neatly assembled in their places. He picked up one of the red knights who sat so solidly on his diminutive horse and smiled whimsically to himself as he glanced across the room at the chattering group. No opponent sat opposite him as he made his first move, the standard white king's pawn to e4. Should he play white or red? He paused for a moment before carefully turning the board round. Red knight to f6, the Alekhine Defence. He was a great admirer of the Russian who many believed was the greatest chess player who ever lived. The Alekhine Defence led to many possible transpositions. Games were often frantic and uncertain. White knight to c3 countered by red pawn to d5. Alekhine's imaginative attacking style appealed to him this evening as he manoeuvred his knights to work together. Yes, tonight he would play red and hope he had the Russian Grandmaster's skill in the endgame.

Chapter 1
Warsaw Perspective

Archie sat behind his heavy, mahogany desk gently cleaning his ear with the sharp end of a pencil. A knock on the door brought him back to the present with a guilty start. Rosemary was always nagging him about his disgusting habits...cleaning his ears while he was thinking, scratching his arse in public and quite unnecessary farting in bed were top of her complaints list, but Rosemary, his wife was at present in England visiting her ghastly mother, so it wasn't her at the door. The new secretary from the communications pool, he vaguely remembered she was called Ruby, poked her head round the door.

'H.E. asked me to let you know that the bag has arrived from London. He wants to open it at 11.30. Do you need to be there?

You bet I need to be there, Archie thought. 'Thank you Ruby.' The girl smiled. Archie smirked back. She was new and he hadn't been certain of her name, but it was a chance worth taking. 'Please tell the Ambassador that it is most important that I be present. I will meet him in his office at 11.30.'

'Very good Captain.' Ruby smiled again and gently closed the door as she left. *Pretty enough*, Archie thought wistfully.

Captain Archibald Ferguson, Naval Attaché to her Majesty's Embassy in Warsaw was expecting two important packages in the *diplomatic bag*. The title diplomatic bag included a whole sealed crate, which the RAF dropped off in Warsaw once a week on their way to the Moscow Embassy. A second bag, the one Archie was concerned with, was a much smaller parcel also delivered by the RAF mainly containing documents. By tradition the Naval Attaché was also head of British espionage in Poland and it was accepted that he should be present when this bag was opened to take responsibility for what the Ambassador called 'secret stuff'. The Ambassador's staff dealt with most of the communications from the Foreign Office, but anything from the Security Services was Archie's domain. One of the packages he was expecting contained nylons, some Max Factor lipstick and a considerable quantity of the ever-popular product from the London Rubber Company, which could not be obtained in Warsaw in 1952. Technically Archie was smuggling, but he justified his actions to himself by reasoning that he needed these to keep his network sweet. There was no need for the Ambassador to be concerned with such things

Archie had already completed three years of his posting. He was aware that Rosemary was vaguely disappointed in his naval career; an undistinguished war followed by appointments that had never been as glamorous as some of his contemporaries. Promotion, by agreeing to go to Warsaw, was a heavy price to pay for both of them. If he kept his nose clean he would only have to do one more year in this awful place. He dreamed of either being transferred back to London or at least somewhere warm. In 1952 Poland had almost no navy thanks to the Russians and no naval officers thanks to the German occupation. Economic life was bleak as Moscow syphoned off most of the country's natural resources and rebuilding

6

of the capital after the devastation of the war was at best half-hearted. What work had been started was in crude communist concrete. He knew Rosemary would extend her stay in England with one excuse after another and he couldn't blame her. There was little for a woman to do locked up in the Embassy and not much more if she ventured outside. Even his espionage work was a joke as London gave him few resources. His overwhelming preoccupation was to prevent Embassy penetration by the Polish Intelligence Service, the *Urzad Bezpieczenstwa,* known helpfully as the UB. They, on the other hand, seemed to have limitless resources and since being taken in hand by the KGB, some highly trained operatives. Archie did not enjoy his job. He picked up his discarded pencil and returned to his twin problems, what to do with his assistant Harry Houghton and the wax in his ear.

Harry had been working as Archie's PA in Warsaw for fourteen months. Apparently, when appointed, he had been the only applicant for the job, which certainly didn't surprise Archie. The two had jogged along reasonably comfortably together, even though Harry couldn't type and was a little too rough and ready for Archie's liking. His war record had been good and he had finished up as Master-at-Arms, about as high as you can get below decks in the British Navy. Rosemary had managed to find a flat for Harry and his wife Peggy when they had first arrived but he acknowledged that the accommodation was pretty basic and the living allowances and salary together did not add up to many luxuries. Archie was not surprised that Peggy had gone home after six months and had obviously no intention of coming back to Warsaw. Rosemary had sympathised with her and Archie hoped that he would be able to persuade his own wife to return after his annual leave in February. The absence of Harry's wife was not in itself Archie's problem, but it certainly compounded it.

For several weeks now Archie had been aware that Harry had developed a strong relationship with a Polish girl called Karytzia. They had met at an Embassy do and Harry had not tried to hide the fact that she was warming his bed at night fairly regularly. The contact had all the hallmarks of a soviet honey trap. Archie thought back to that evening with some embarrassment. In Rosemary's absence and with far too much vodka inside him, he had snogged with another attractive Pole whose name he couldn't even remember. He had been saved from making a complete fool of himself by a tap on the shoulder and an urgent telephone message from London. When he recalled the incident next morning he had little doubt that the girl in question had been an agent for the UB, trying to compromise him. Archie expected that Harry's Karytzia was also in the employ of the UB, but as Harry had almost no contact with secret information this had not disturbed him unduly. There was almost nothing of any value on the secret list anyway. A bigger concern was recent information that Harry was involved in extensive smuggling using his diplomatic status as cover. Though evidence was skimpy one of his sources gave information about a lucrative trade in coffee and medicines organised from Harry's flat. Archie convinced himself that this was a more serious matter than his own professional dabbling in condoms and nylons. In addition Harry was drinking too much. It was time for him to return to England and he decided to tell him so that afternoon.

When Archie eventually spoke to Harry and informed him of his imminent transfer home it had all gone remarkably smoothly. There had been no mention of Polish mistresses, illicit trading or drink. The given reason was a need to reorganise the office and because of administrative cut-backs, to replace Harry with a cheaper unmarried secretary. Harry had not seemed particularly surprised and his only question was a request for a reasonable reference to the Naval Appointments Board so that he could get another job. This Archie was only too pleased to do. 'I know Vic Pennells, the Assistant to the Director, very well,' he told Harry. 'We were in the same house at Harrow, and he regularly comes to stay with Rosemary and me at our house in Hampshire. I own the fishing on a stretch of the Test which in my opinion is as good as anywhere in the South of England. Vic will see you right.'

Harry could not give a damn what the fishing was like on the Test or any other river for that matter. He desparately needed Captain Archie Bloody Ferguson to give him a clean reference and security clearance so he could get another job. At 46 with little formal education he was hardly an employment catch.

Karytzia was waiting for him when he returned to his scruffy little flat later that evening. She seemed genuinely upset when he told her his news and wept in his arms repeating how much she loved him.

'And I love you too,' Harry comforted her.

'Please take me to England with you,' Karytzia begged him.

'Of course I will Kara darling.' Up to that moment the idea hadn't crossed Harry's mind. He was comfortable enough in their energetic and casual sex life in Warsaw, but the more he thought about it, the idea of exchanging Peggy's cold tolerance of him with Kara's passionate enthusiasm on a more permanent basis appealed. Harry was not one for thinking things through very carefully but this idea showed promise. 'Of course I will darling. As soon as I get settled in England I will send for you, I promise.' Karytzia stopped crying and began to unbutton Harry's trousers. Harry immediately stopped worrying about the consequences of a decision so lightly taken.

Next morning when Karytzia reported to her controller in the UB, she was congratulated on a job well done and promised another assignment shortly. 'There may be some loose ends to tie up,' the Colonel told her, 'then you can take some leave. Most of the correspondence that usually follows something like this, we can cope with.'

So it was that a thoroughly compromised chancer, part time informant and blackmarketeer returned to England with a glowing reference from the Embassy in Warsaw seeking further employment with the Admiralty.

Chapter 2
New Opportunities

Victor Pennells, Civil Assistant to the Director of Naval Intelligence, picked up the top file from the pile on his desk. He just had time to squeeze in his fifth candidate before lunch. If he could deal with the man quickly he had a good chance of reaching the Clarendon Arms before the rest of the office. Pennells was proud of his ability to fit the right man in the right job. He knew his reputation for 'soundness' was one of his strengths. With luck there would be two more promotions inside the Admiralty before retirement. He opened the file to refresh his memory.

HENRY FREDERICK HOUGHTON

Yes this was the one Archie had recommended from Warsaw, ex Master-at-Arms with a solid reputation from the war. He glanced at the photograph on the inside of the front cover. If true to type he would be well turned out, used to giving and taking orders, probably slightly overweight and not lacking in self confidence. He had three possible vacancies any of which might suit Mr Houghton; a stores job in Portsmouth, barracks manager in Plymouth or filing clerk in Portland. He would not make up his mind till he had met the candidate.

Harry knew what was expected from him. He was not particularly nervous about the interview to come. *What will be, will be* he thought. He had spent his life managing people like Pennells. That morning he had shaved off the moustache he had grown in Poland and paid for a good haircut. Appearance was important and his best suit had the right patina of age...clean but not flashy. He would be confident yet not cocky, courteous but not crawling and above all no humour. The Navy didn't like humour. Jokes could only go down ranks never up. There were questions about Poland he might have difficulty in answering truthfully, but he was not against lying so long as he wasn't found out. After all everyone did it at interviews. He had sneaked a look at the reference Captain Ferguson had written for him. There was nothing in that which would lessen his chances. In fact he was quite proud of the paper character portrayed. He needed a job badly. He had returned from Warsaw with a substantial nest egg, but it was surprising how quickly he was eating into his capital.

Victor Pennells almost immediately decided that Portland was the right place for Houghton. He wouldn't even bother to mention the other possibilities. 'There is a position I think might suit you at the Underwater Detection Establishment which is adjacent to the naval base in Portland. That is Portland, Dorset not Portland, Oregon.' He laughed at his own joke and Harry dutifully smiled. 'The UDE is a vital secret Admiralty establishment responsible for all our research into submarine warfare. Since they moved back from Scotland five years ago numbers of staff have been growing and they have requested additional help in the office; a filing clerk. It's not much of a job at present and I'm afraid the salary is nothing to write home about, but if you keep your nose clean I am sure you will quickly rise like cream to the top.' He snorted again at his joke noticing at the same time that Harry's complexion was far from cream-like and his mottled face and over red nose suggested the possibility of a drink problem. This was not uncommon in the Navy. A scintilla of doubt crossed his mind, but then Archie hadn't mentioned any difficulties in his reference, so he let the doubt slip quietly away. 'Is this the sort of position that might suit you?'

Harry was ready to leap at any job. His reply was carefully moderated. 'I am sure it's something I can manage easily enough sir. I had a more responsible position in Warsaw, but I will be pleased to work again in England, and I am sure I can work my way up to promotion.' *That seemed to go down well enough with Pennells*, Harry thought. 'My wife didn't like Poland and returned to England some months ago. We will be able to set up home together again in Dorset. She has a daughter, Margaret, in Portsmouth who she likes to visit. I am pleased to accept your offer sir.'

'That's that then.' Pennells would get his early lunch after all. 'I will send you the details and a travel warrant by post. Where are you staying?'

'Victory Services Club at Marble Arch Sir. And thank you for your help.' Harry rose from his chair. He was as anxious as Pennells to end the interview.'

'Oh, just a thought Mr Houghton,' Victor Pennells said stretching out his hand, 'you will need security clearance. After all the Portland base is a pretty sensitive area.'

'That's all right sir. I had full clearance in Warsaw.' So Harry Houghton, who in his previous job had been happy to sell on any information he'd gleaned, found himself employed in the heart of the Navy's most secret research establishment.

Chapter 3
Who is Gordon Lonsdale?

His mother, Olga Bousa, registered Gordon Arnold Lonsdale's birth in Calgary, Canada in August 1931. He was aged eight. Gordon had been born in Cobalt, Ontario on August 27th 1924, the son of a miner Emmanuel Lonsdale and a Finnish mother. By 1931 Olga had left Gordon's father and wished to return to her native Finland with her young son and a new man in her life. She needed a passport and thus the registration. The young child and his mother left Canada in the autumn of 1931.

In the spring of 1954 a Gordon Lonsdale disembarked from a Russian merchant ship in Vancouver harbour. A problem undetected by the authorities as he passed through immigration was that the young Gordon had been circumcised as a baby. Gordon aged 30 had his foreskin intact. No one, except possibly some ancient KGB officer, knows what happened to the young Gordon in Finland. His existence has been wiped from the pages of history. But undoubtedly the soviet authorities found his details in Finland's public records, which they captured during the war. The Gordon Lonsdale who found lodgings in the dock area of Vancouver was a brilliant soviet naval officer whose real name was Konon Molody. He was to become one of the Soviet Union's most successful spies.

Lonsdale, as he must now be called, was hugely excited by his first foreign assignment. His training in Moscow was intense and thorough. As well as

Russian, he spoke fluent Finnish some Polish and accentless English. Lonsdale was one of the new school of soviet spies with clear instruction from the KGB. No longer was spying to be managed through foreign embassies, with agents easily identified by national security services. Lonsdale was to be part of a network of illegal residents established in all 'enemy' countries. The risks for these agents were high. If discovered there was to be no diplomatic immunity followed by a flight home in disgrace as invariably happened to embassy staff. Illegal residents would have to take their chances in the law courts. On the other hand the rewards were considerable. An effective 'illegal' had a freedom of action and access to a wide range of potential sources that could never be the privilege of embassy staffers. Lonsdale's instruction was first to consolidate his backstory in Canada so that it could never be challenged successfully. He was to base himself in Toronto and immerse himself in North American life so that being Gordon Lonsdale, Canadian citizen, became second nature to him. Lonsdale already had a brilliant aptitude for languages. Now he was to develop a Canadian accent that would be flawless. When he was confident in his new persona he was to move to New York where the Rezidentura would brief him further.

As his instructors had taught him, Lonsdale settled into a small bed-sit run by a member of the Canadian communist party. He took a local bus from the dock area to the Vancouver train station and in the name of Gordon Lonsdale booked a seat to Toronto on *The Canadian* for the following Friday. Moscow reckoned the four days and 4,500 kilometre train journey across Canada would give him time to get used to his new environment with fewer chances of making mistakes. With his ticket satisfactorily booked he returned to his safe-house, followed his silent host up the stairs to the small bedroom and threw himself onto the bed, able to relax for the first time since he had landed.

Lonsdale's controller had warned him that the first few days of a new assignment were among the most critical. For 12 hours he stayed in his room building up his determination to go out into the streets of Vancouver. On his second day, as it was getting dark, he braved the late spring flurry of sleet and took a trolley bus downtown to the city centre. He knew he had been well trained in Moscow, but there was a world of difference between a training run in the streets of his home town and the real thing. He looked around the crowded bus. No one was paying him particular attention. He saw only tired people returning home after a day's work. He searched for the alert eyes of a watcher; something he had quickly learned to recognise at home. Nothing. Casual strangers chatted to each other in a desultory way. He had been warned to expect this in a free society; so different from the tense silence of Moscow. The large lady squashed in the seat next to him passed a comment about the weather. *Has it been raining a lot recently in Vancouver?* He had no idea. He mumbled a reply suggesting his shoes were unsuitable for the wet. It seemed to satisfy her but he was aware that he could already have inadvertently drawn attention to himself. He decided to get off at the next halt.

Out of the many garish bars to choose from Lonsdale went into the *Lamplighter* solely because he liked the name. He found an empty seat at a corner table and systematically began to study the company. This was the society he had to assimilate into…the society he was supposed to have grown up in. He was 32 years old, well built, handsome and with money in his pocket. Inadvertently he had found himself in one of Vancouver's bars frequented by the unmarried. It was only a few minutes before a pretty girl, Lonsdale guessed she was in her mid- to late-twenties, plonked herself in the seat next to him. 'Hi, I'm Eugenie.'

'Hi, my name is Gordon.' Lonsdale knew he was attractive to women. He never had any difficultly picking them up and he enjoyed sex. His heart however was constant to his wife Galina back home. She had told him that it was easy for girls to fall for his charm and had no expectations that he would be sexually faithful to her while he was away. She knew that he would always come home to her and their little son eventually. She had no difficulty in being faithful to him. 'Would you like a drink?' he asked.

'First time here?' Eugenie looked at him quizzically. 'Everyone buys their own in the *Lamplighter*.'

Lonsdale laughed. 'Worth a try,' he said. He then asked Eugenie about herself. He quickly learned that her friends called her Genie and from then on it was easy. They chatted in a relaxed way for the best part of an hour and Lonsdale learned about her family, her job and her supervisor who was apparently 'a real jerk'. From Gordon she learned the backstory he had so thoroughly prepared. None of it caused any alarms.

'Do you want to go somewhere else Gordon?' He had expected the question for some time.

'You mean another bar or a club?' He studied his beer bottle on the table.

'Or you could come round to my place. My flat is only ten minutes walk.'

Lonsdale looked up at her face. She was extremely pretty, warm and available. His body was aching for the relief of casual sex, something that had not been accessible to him for weeks. He smiled and Genie knew she was wanted. 'Sorry.' He took hold of her hands and shook his head. 'I can't tonight. I have to be somewhere. Perhaps we can meet again another night.'

The rejection was gentle and the future sounded like a possibility. They parted as friends and Lonsdale returned to his dingy bed-sit pleased by how well things had gone. Next day he would catch the Canadian on what the pamphlet described as the most stunning train journey in the world.

Chapter 4
New York

He spent 8 weeks in Toronto before he was ready to move to the United States. Lonsdale felt remarkably cheerful as the Greyhound bus approached the Port Authority Bus terminal in New York. The day before he had been mildly concerned about the first leg of his journey from Toronto to Detroit, but he had crossed the border into the US with no trouble from immigration. He thought over what he had achieved so far. For his time in Toronto he had rented a flat. This had given him the address he needed to obtain some of his documents. The passport created for him in Moscow, had enabled him to acquire his Canadian Social Insurance Number. He had successfully passed his driving test and was the possessor of a Canadian driving licence. As part of his background research he had hired a car and taken the 5-hour trip to Cobalt to visit the site of his borrowed early life and the grave of his assumed father. He had been fortunate to be taken on as a temporary worker in the head office Sun Life Assurance Company. He had regularly chatted to local Canadians and despite a few minor slips he was confident that if challenged he could now pass as a Canadian citizen with a working knowledge of Toronto. Now he was nearing New York. He was nervous about his next meeting, but he thought it unlikely he could be faulted on his achievements so far.

For 18 hours Lonsdale kept the entrance to the block of flats in Fulton Street, Lower Manhattan, under observation. Part of his meticulously training by the KGB for the last two years had focussed on not underestimating the skills of his opponents the American FBI. There was no evidence of other watchers. He was ready to meet William Fisher, for the first time. Fisher, later know to the FBI as Colonel Rudolph Abel, was *Rezidentura* and head of the Soviet spy ring in America.

The scholarly man who greeted him at the door of his fifth floor art studio was no-one's idea of a spy. Fisher, bald and bespectacled, seemed older than his 50 years, and somewhat frail. Gordon was not fooled. From 1949 William Fisher had founded and controlled the 'Volunteer' spy ring that had squeezed America's atomic secrets out of Los Alamos. The two exchanged the signs and countersigns agreed by Moscow Centre and Lonsdale entered the studio. Looking round he quickly realised how thoroughly Fisher had immersed himself in his cover as artist and photographer. He formally introduced himself in Russian. 'I am Konon Trofimovich Molody, Colonel.'

Fisher at first said nothing, staring at him with eyes that were flat and cold. They reminded Gordon of the eyes of a carp he had caught with his father. As it lay on the floorboards of his rowing boat, dying, it stared in just such a cold accusing manner. He shivered as he waited for Fisher to speak.

'Has Moscow taught you nothing?' He spoke in English. There was almost no trace of a foreign accent, but also no trace of friendliness in the voice. 'You will never again use that name outside Russia. You are to live and breathe as Gordon Lonsdale. Yes, this is at first a lie, but you must live the lie until the lie becomes the truth. It is better that you never use the Russian language except in communications with Moscow.' His eyes hooded like a hawk and Lonsdale cursed himself for making such an elementary mistake. 'Also you will never again call me Colonel. My name is William Fisher and if you need to refer to me in documents, my code name is ALEC. Yours will be MARK. If you wish to survive as an illegal you must not just think the role, you must live it, be it. Is that clear?' Fisher waved Gordon Lonsdale to a chair and continued to pace up and down.

'Reports on you from Moscow are excellent. For the next five years the work you will undertake is of vital importance to the Motherland. You will rarely see your wife and child. You are ready for that?' Of course he was ready. Lonsdale prepared a suitable reply but Fisher didn't wait for an answer. 'You will lose yourself into New York life for the next six months. You will be working for me. I am told you are expert in communications. I need your help in setting up a new organisation. Things have been quiet here as my previous assistants are no longer in the United States. I believe our old system to be compromised. At the end of that time you will be going to England. Prepare yourself and find a trade.' For the next half hour Fisher instructed Lonsdale in code signs, radio frequencies and dead letter drops. He handed over a fat envelope. 'There are enough dollars in here to keep you going while you are in New York. You will not come to this address again even in emergency. I have told you how to make contact with me. I wish you well.' Fisher ushered him to the door.

Lonsdale had hardly spoken a word throughout the whole meeting. He slowly walked down the stairs into the New York traffic aware that he was setting off on a life of loneliness and deceit. He was like a pistol, primed and loaded, waiting for someone to pull the trigger. He believed Fisher was the man to do that. Far from being daunted by his mission, the idea excited him.

Chapter 5
Bedding In

Harry knew he was lucky to get the job at Portland. A whiff of a single one of the multitude of little scams he had controlled in Warsaw would have been enough to get him instantly dismissed from a top secret Admiralty establishment. But he quickly recognized that security at Portland was a joke.

He had tried to show interest as a young, pasty-faced lieutenant, spotty with a plummy accent, gave him a brief history lesson as part of his induction. 'It was here in 1927 that the ASDIC system for detecting submarines using sound waves was first developed. The very name ASDIC was a bit of a joke by their Lordships at Admiralty House to disguise the fact that sound location was being used.' He laughed with an uncomfortable *hee-haw* that would have embarrassed Harry if he had been paying attention. A shapely female leg showing round the door of the next office had momentarily distracted him. 'The Admirals claimed in a press release that ASDIC stood for Anti Submarine Detection Investigation Committee, though no such committee actually existed.' He *hee-hawed* again, though Harry was at a loss to see anything remotely funny in any of this. 'During the war the Underwater Detection Establishment moved up to Dunoon on the Clyde, to avoid the bombs, but we moved back here in 1947.' He smiled graciously to Harry as if all this had been the result of his own mighty endeavours. 'Here we are the centre for all research into submarine warfare in Britain.'

'What will I be doing?' Harry put on his best quizzical, please-instruct-me-further, face. He suspected he already knew the answer to this, no doubt he would be pushing paper from one tray to another, but there would be no harm in giving the appearance of keenness to this twit. 'I am anxious to get things right. I don't want to mess up.'

'There's no fear of that;' another half hee-haw accompanied by a strangled snort. 'I'm here to keep an eye on you.'

Harry smiled graciously. *If this baby lieutenant is a measure of the security at the base, I reckon there will be plenty of opportunities for extra-curricular activities.*

One problem that he could not smile away was his wife Peggy. Reluctantly she had agreed to set up house with him in a small, two bedroomed house in Weymouth. Both quickly recognized that they now had very little interest in each other. Harry's attempts at intimacy had been coldly rebuffed and they spoke less and less. With increased frequency Peggy visited her daughter Margaret in Gosport. Margaret was married to a naval officer who made no attempt to hide his dislike of Harry. It became obvious that he was not welcome in their home. As Peggy spent more and more time with them in Portsmouth Harry contentedly slipped into a comfortable bachelor existence.

When he first arrived in England he had written to Karytzia in Warsaw, expressing his love and repeating his vague promise to try to get her a visa and bring her to England. Her replies were addressed to the Post Office in Broadwey so that Peggy could not accidentally stumble on them. Harry sent a few parcels with stockings and cosmetics to Poland, which Kara joyfully acknowledged, at the same time pleading with him to help her escape. Her letters encouraged in Harry a delightful fantasy of living together with her in Dorset. He held her letters to his nose inhaling a remembrance of their energetic sex life. At these moments he knew his marriage to Peggy was drifting to a close, but he was too indolent to do anything about it.

Chapter 6
Peggy

Being married to Harry hadn't been much fun for Peggy Houghton. By 55 she had aged badly having a crumpled appearance and a sour bitter face. Peggy was not the sort of person that strangers naturally would wish to come up to talk to. She was bitter at the hand life had dealt her. She would admit to herself that she had married Harry to gain security for herself and her young daughter Margaret after the failure of her first marriage but Harry was a disappointment. There had been little love between them and she recognized in Harry a dishonest chancer who paid scant attention to truth and honour. The war hero and loveable rogue she thought she had married turned out to be just a rogue. Her short unhappy stay in Warsaw had effectively ended their relationship and Harry's attempts to involve her in his 'little money-making schemes,' had cemented her distrust and contempt for him.

His effort to revive marital life in Weymouth was short lived and doomed to failure. She quickly suspected that much of Harry's correspondence from Warsaw was not with old work colleagues as he claimed and she guessed that it wouldn't be long before he was again engaged in activities, which were of doubtful legality. Peggy knew Harry was unlikely to take any action with regard to their marriage, but when during one of her prolonged stays in Gosport, Margaret invited her to live with her and her husband on a permanent basis she decided to take the initiative. She drove from her daughter's home to the little cottage in Weymouth to collect the few belongings that she had left there. By deliberately choosing a time when she knew Harry would be at work she hoped to avoid fuss. In case she met neighbours she dressed smartly in her best navy blue suit and, as a gesture of her coming independence, wore her new cream mushroom hat recently made popular by Mr Dior. The overall effect was a little confused and slightly comical, but dressing up made her feel more self-confident than she had for some time. She had no intention of telling Harry she was coming nor leaving him a note that she had been. For the last time she opened the cottage door with her own key.

Peggy was scrupulously honest in what she took. She emptied her wardrobe upstairs, removed exactly half of the photographs that were relevant to their marriage and packed up the mahogany card table, which was their one genuine antique, but had been a wedding gift from her first husband. Though she knew many of the hidey-holes where Harry had cash secreted, some of them tins buried in the garden, she ignored these correctly suspecting that this money was produced by illegal activities. She could however not resist looking at the contents of Harry's desk. The opened letter from Karitzia in Warsaw left her in no doubt as to the nature of their relationship. She was embarrassed and humiliated by the explicit description of their sexual activities. Kara's final plea for Harry to hurry up and secure her visa for England left her in no doubt what his ultimate intentions were. Seething with anger she searched further. She carefully opened a brown envelope she found in the top drawer of the bureau. Admiralty plans and pamphlets spilled out onto the desk. None of them was marked *Top Secret*, but she could see no reason for a filing clerk to have these hidden in his home. She had been aware of some of Harry's illegal activities in Warsaw and guessed he was already up to his old tricks again. Peggy convinced herself that it was her patriotic duty to let the authorities know of his little schemes, but deep down she knew that it was jealousy over his liaison with Karitzia, which prompted her next action. She carefully placed the incriminating documents back in the drawer and, returning Kara's letter to its envelope, hid it under the detritus on Harry's desk.

At the gates of the UWE she asked the guard if she could speak to the security officer. She was escorted to a small room adjacent to the guardhouse and reported all she knew and some of what she guessed. The security officer carefully noted down everything she told him even asking how to spell Karitzia's name. He recorded that she was 55 years old, currently living with a daughter in Gosport and listed all her complaints. When the interview was finished he escorted her back to the main gate, promising that the matter would be fully investigated. Peggy left in a glow of self-righteous satisfaction. That would teach Harry to mess around.

The Head of Security knew Harry and was aware that he had no contact with secret information, but decided that the matter was potentially too serious for him to deal with. He sent a report to the Head of Naval Security in London who routinely readdressed it to C Branch of MI5 where it landed on the desk of a young officer called Duncan Waugh. Waugh read the report from Portland and looking up Houghton in the MI5 Registry found no reference to him. The same day he wrote a memorandum for the Head of C Branch.

This morning a flimsy from Admiralty Security landed on my desk. Last week the navy security officer at the Underwater Weapons Establishment on Portland received an oral complaint against one of the staff of UWE. Apparently a middle-aged lady in some state of agitation had reported to the officer on the main gate that her husband Harry Houghton had secret documents at their cottage in Weymouth. Her story was that she mistakenly opened a parcel wrapped in brown paper, which must have belonged to Houghton. It contained Admiralty papers. She also claimed that he occasionally made trips to London where he met foreigners who she felt sure were communist. As further proof of guilt her husband had a considerable sum of money hidden in a tin in the garden. She felt it was her patriotic duty to report this. Admiralty have passed the problem to us.

Henry Frederick Houghton has been employed at Portland since 1952 in a minor administrative capacity. For 18 months he was assistant to our naval attaché in Warsaw and before that he served in the navy during the war until he left the service in 1950 with the rank of Master-at-Arms. There are no official complaints against him though he did leave Warsaw sooner than expected after trouble with a woman. At no times does Houghton have access to confidential documents.

The lady who made the report is Mrs Peggy Houghton who is presently estranged from her husband. There was a complaint of domestic abuse from her in January 1952. The reason given then was Houghton's excessive drinking. This complaint was not substantiated. Mrs Houghton left Warsaw and no action was taken. Portland Security affirms that Houghton might be in a relationship with a local girl who also works at the UWE. The Officer i/c believes Mrs Houghton's complaint is a typical malicious accusation by a deserted wife and/or the fantasy of a menopausal middle-aged woman.

As Portland also confirms Houghton has no access to secret material, I conclude that the Portland Security Officer is correct in his assessment and I recommend that no further action be taken.

The memorandum was signed by Duncan Waugh, counter signed by Head of C Branch, filed and forgotten. An appropriate reply was sent to Portland.

Chapter 7
Genesis of a Spy

When Peggy moved out, living on his own in the cottage in Weymouth seemed like a waste of money to Harry. With a flash of inspiration, as ill thought through as most of his plans, he handed in notice to his landlord and bought a second-hand caravan, advertised in the Dorset Evening Echo. To call the caravan second-hand was to flatter it. Several previous owners had each contributed various levels of skill to its maintenance, and the dull olive green paint on the outside was the only uniform feature about it. There was an electric powered shower inside which worked intermittently, a chemical toilet and a small Calor Gas stove. A previous owner had built a bunk bed at the tow-bar end and Harry worked out that if required, he could make a double bed out of the table and two side bunks. He guessed he would be fine in the summer but had a suspicion of doubt as to whether he would be warm enough in winter. With sufficient cash saved from Warsaw (thank you coffee and nylons) the cost of the caravan hardly made a dent in his capital.

Harry persuaded the garage owner who was selling the caravan to tow it to a site he had found on the Abbotsbury Road. He quickly discovered that this was too open to the public gaze for his liking. A second move to Bowleaze Cove also proved to be unsatisfactory. Eventually he found a site on the eastern side of the Isle of Portland that was suitably discreet with the added advantage of free electricity when he ran an electric cable to a spare socket in the lavatory block. He doubted if he would be doing much entertaining in his caravan, but its Spartan disrepair suited him.

The local girl mentioned in Duncan Waugh's report to his boss was Ethel Gee. Ethel, known in her family as Bunty, worked in the next office to Harry and over the summer months their relationship was little more than trips out in his car at week-ends or after-work drinks usually in the Elm Tree pub in Langton Herring. On a particular Wednesday in July Harry poked his head round the door of the office in which Ethel was working. He coughed to attract her attention. 'Sorry Old Girl, can't manage this Saturday. Have to go to London after work on Friday.' He gave her a friendly wave and disappeared down the corridor.

Ethel tried hard to hide her disappointment at Harry's casually delivered news. After all it wasn't as if he was cancelling a date. It was just a trip to Thomas Hardy's cottage, which she had planned for them. Now the prospect would be a weekend nursing Aunt Angela and looking after mother. Life didn't contain much joy for Ethel. She had been born and raised on Portland but had eventually escaped the confines of a dour, strict family to work in the office of an aircraft factory in Hamble. Five years before, a telephone call from her mother had warned her that her father had just had a heart attack. Perhaps Ethel would think of coming home. She could see at once that any freedom she might have acquired was ending. The idea of living back in Portland made her feel sick. When her father died a few months later she knew there was little option for her. An advert, interview and position for a temporary filing clerk at the Underwater Weapons Establishment gave her a small income, and before long temporary had stretched into semi-permanent. Mother invited her own invalid sister Angela and husband John to share her house and gradually Ethel had found herself as an unpaid carer for three decrepit pensioners. Uncle John particularly irritated her, sitting in father's chair ordering her about. 'Bunty, pour me a glass of beer,' and 'Bunty, fetch my slippers.' She remembered with bitterness when he had told her how lucky she was to have a family to look after her now that she was too old to get married. There was little she could do to stop her life getting narrower and narrower. Sometimes she had to go to her bedroom and bite her wrist to stop herself screaming at them.

Ethel knew Uncle John was probably right about marriage. She was 41, quite plain and spinsterish. She had girl friends at work but never seemed to have the time or energy to do things with them. She had resigned herself to a life of domestic drudgery when Harry moved into the next office. Everyone liked Harry. He was cheerful, and ready to tease all the girls in the office. He had a fund of risqué jokes and a casual disregard for authority, which gave Ethel a frisson of excitement. Their first personal contact was when he had sat down next to her in the canteen at lunch. He had told her some of his personal history, not disguising the fact that he was married but confided that his wife and daughter lived apart from him in Gosport. Four or five lunches later he had invited her for a ride in his new car. She had decided not to tell her mother this, as she would certainly have disapproved. Nor did she mention that they had gone for a drink later. Harry told her that he did not consider himself married but Ethel knew that would not count with the strict Baptist Mrs Gee. She enjoyed her little trips with Harry and was coming to accept that Harry enjoyed her company as well. The cancelled arrangement for Saturday upset Ethel considerably, but Harry set off for London with a feeling of anticipation.

The reason for Harry's sudden trip to London was a mysterious telephone call he received one day at work. The caller, George claimed to be an acquaintance from Warsaw, though Harry had no recollection of him. George had a message from Karitzia, which he needed to pass on to Harry personally. The mention of Kara's name rekindled his feelings for her and was sufficient to get him on the evening train from Weymouth, though he remained sceptical that the outcome of his trip would be a happy one. When Harry met George in the lobby of the Dulwich Art Gallery it was obvious to him almost immediately that there would be no good news about Karitzia. George, a nervous middle-aged man in a jacket and tie, quickly admitted he had never been to Poland and Harry guessed he was a UB plant. Kara was just the juicy bait for this little fishing trip. Once Harry had worked this out, he was confident he could manage the Georges of this world easily enough. There was a vague hint of cockney in George's spoken English, but Harry could find few clues to his social background.

'Your friend Karitzia is now considered 'politically unreliable' he told Harry. You've been writing to her and sending her parcels which is enough to make people over there suspicious. If you want to get her a visa it'll only be possible in exchange for certain bits of information required by the Polish government. They specifically want to know the movement of Navy ships in and out of Portland Harbour.' As Harry knew this was published regularly at the UDE in a broadsheet called the *Daily State*, he readily agreed to play along and George set up a complicated communication channel so Harry could send the information to London. He thought wistfully that this was unlikely to have any effect on whether Kara obtained a visa or not, but as it was not illegal, he was enough of an optimist to have a go. Over the next few months he sent off what the Poles requested. After the Dulwich meeting Harry never saw George again.

One evening in the late summer there was a knock on the caravan door and Harry met Nikki for the first time. He introduced himself and entered before Harry had a chance to invite him in. Nikki's personality dominated the tiny room though he was not physically a large man. From his smart suit and serious manner and just a hint of a mid-European accent Harry guessed that Nikki was more likely to be Russian than Polish, and if he was Russian he was likely to be KGB. Harry's usefulness had been passed along the line and from that moment he had nothing further to do with the Poles. Nikki was very different from George. There was a steeliness in him that occasionally he tried to disguise with a friendly smile. This made Harry wary. Nikki wouldn't be managed as Harry had managed George. He thanked Harry for the information that he had already sent and said he needed to know when the army ranges at Lulworth would practise firing out to sea. This information was published daily in the Dorset Evening Echo in a section called 'Notice to Mariners', to help the Weymouth fishing fleet steer well clear, so Harry had no problems agreeing. That apparently was that and Nikki rose to leave. 'I won't be coming here again. I would like to see you next Saturday at six in the evening at the Toby Jug on the Kingston bypass.' He fished in his coat pocket, pulling out a brown envelope. 'This is for your travel expenses.' He lobbed it onto the table, not giving Harry an opportunity to refuse. The envelope was suitably fat.

All subsequent meetings with Nikki were in London usually in pubs and invariably a different place each time. After two or three meetings both Harry and Nikki dropped the pretence that this was anything other than spying, though the information Harry supplied continued to be banal and usually readily available to the public. When asked which areas of the Channel had been allocated to the Navy for exercises Harry simply put his name down for a regular extra copy of the *Daily State* and sent it on to an address Nikki supplied. At the end of each meeting Nikki would drop an envelope onto the pub table. 'For expenses,' he would say with a shrug and a smile. Harry was pleased to note that his expenses were getting heavier.

It was Nikki who taught Harry some of the basic skills of spying. He produced a bunch of brochures, one for the Scotch House, a second for Hoover cleaners and a third from Prudential

Assurance with several others. Each of them represented a different meeting place and somewhere inside the one posted to Harry there would be a couple of pinholes which would show date and time. He gave Harry a tiny Russian Minox camera, about the size of a cigarette lighter and taught him how to use it. 'It might be useful later on,' was the only clue for Harry that things might get more serious. For the time being he was being well paid for useless information and he found the cloak and dagger stuff exciting.

Nikki recognized Harry's need for thrill and adventure and started to use him on different missions. On one occasion he was to collect a parcel sellotaped behind the door in a public lavatory in Alresford, which was next to the police station. Harry was to take the parcel to the Bunch of Grapes in the Brompton Road. At the left hand end of the bar a man would be would be waiting for him. Harry stood in the pub doorway scanning the room. No one paid him any attention. The man sitting on a bar stool to the left was obviously his contact. He had his head down, buried in a book, but a carefully folded copy of The Daily Herald was sticking out of his raincoat pocket. Harry had been told to expect this. The man had the appearance of a bookie's runner or Harry mischievously thought, a cartoon spy. He ordered himself a beer and sat down next to the man. 'Is that the evening paper?' he asked pointing at The Herald

The man's proper response was, 'No. I'm afraid it is only a daily.'

Harry would counter with 'I only wanted to see the racing results,' and then hand over the parcel in the pub lavatory. Though Harry met this contact on several occasions in different pubs they never spoke apart from these three sentences. Why all this rigmarole was necessary Harry could not guess, but he did wonder if his reliability was being tested. He didn't mind though as a major result of all these expedition was even fatter expenses. There was never any mention of Karitzia.

After some months of playing these little games Nikki began to turn up the heat. He found it difficult to accept that Harry couldn't easily lay his hands on top-secret information. Harry tried explaining that even when he was transferred to the Port Auxiliary Repair Unit and became sole filing clerk he rarely came into contact with confidential material. Harry found the increased pressure uncomfortable and decided to ignore two of the appointment brochures that arrived. He was congratulating himself on retaining the upper hand when a couple of East End thugs turned up at the caravan and beat him up. They were careful enough to leave his face unmarked but systematically kicked and punched the rest of his body. A parting message delivered with a final kick was that there would be another doing over if he ignored the next summons and that his new girl friend Miss Gee would also suffer. There was no way Harry could go to the police. He would certainly lose his job and might even have already committed enough of a crime to go to prison. When the brochure for the new Renault car arrived he decided to meet with Nikki as ordered. Nikki was very warm and welcoming with no mention of either the missed meetings or the thugs visit. He handed over a bonus of £200. Harry knew he was in too deep now to get out. He would go on with what they wanted if only to protect himself and Ethel.

A second Russian, who introduced himself as Roman, came occasionally to visit Harry on Portland. He was altogether more frightening than Nikki and from his manner it was obvious he was not used to being disobeyed. From his comments Harry learned that he was higher up the soviet/KGB food chain than Nikki, but he was discouraged from asking personal questions. Roman's technical questions and knowledge of naval matters suggested to Harry that he had been a sailor. If this was correct, he guessed Roman would have been a reasonably senior officer. On one occasion Roman lost his temper saying that his bosses were very dissatisfied with the quality of material Harry was providing. He tried to bluff it out explaining that it was a problem easily trying to lay his hands on secret material from his present job. Rashly he told Roman not to worry and assured him that he would find a way. For the first time Harry wondered if he might need Ethel's help. She worked in the next office in the UDE and most likely had access to all the secret test trials that the Admiralty was doing in Portland Harbour. She was always pretty discreet about her work, but through casual remarks and hints, he had a good idea what she did and what she knew. He wasn't sure how much the Russians knew about his personal life and chose not to mention Ethel to Roman.

It was Roman who paid for Harry's skiing holiday in Austria. In return all he had to do was to meet a contact in the Alte Poste Hotel in Mayerhofen, and it was Roman who arranged for him to meet Tony in Gresham's Hotel in Dublin. Tony was the most sinister of all the Russians Harry met... not so much as what he said but in the way he looked and his long silences. He wanted diagrams of the Portland Dockyards and details about night-time security there. He told Harry it was rare for him to meet even with his top operatives in the field to preserve his anonymity. He suggested it was an honour that he chose to meet with Harry at all. After Tony had gone Harry worked out that he was probably the director of operations for the KGB in England or even the whole of Europe and perhaps the paymaster of all the spies.

The strangest job Harry did for Roman was picking up two Russian agents from a submarine lying off Portland. He had already identified Church Ope Cove on the east coast of the island as the best place for a landing...not near authorities in Portland Harbour and out of sight of coastguards at Portland Bill. The cove was also near his caravan site, which in an emergency could act as a safe haven. Roman gave detailed instructions. Harry was to place two red leading lights on a cliff top at a time he would indicate later. On the night in question Harry was to take a drink in the Elm Tree (not in itself a hardship) and Roman would telephone pretending to be his cousin. The time of his train arriving in Dorchester would be the time Harry had to switch on the lights. The first night he waited for two hours on the beach but nothing happened. The second night at about eleven o'clock a small boat scrunched onto the pebbles.

41

'Did you get any fish?' This was the agreed password.

'None at all.' This was to be the counter signal.

'What a pity.' Harry's signal that all was clear.

Two silent passengers stepped onto the shore and the little dinghy pushed quickly and quietly away. He led the two Russians (he assumed they were Russians though they never spoke another word the whole time he was with them) to the car he had parked on the cliff top. As they drove to the edge of the causeway leading off Portland they were stopped at a police checkpoint. The Russians tried to slide down into the foot well to hide, but a cheerful Harry told them they must relax and act normally. He knew the sirens meant that a convict had escaped from one of the many prisons on the island – quite a common occurrence. The police would have a detailed description of the escapee so Harry was unconcerned. This experience gave him a real buzz, confident that the police would just look in the car, but he particularly enjoyed the scared behaviour of the two professional soviet spies. Throughout the journey neither of them spoke even to say thank you. When they arrived at Blandford Forum railway station as per Roman's instructions, Harry pushed them out into the car park. He never saw them again and didn't care much what happened to them. A week later he received an envelope containing £200 but no letter.

By now Harry realised that for the memory of Karitzia, and a quiver of remembered sexual satisfaction he was now hopelessly in the thrall of his soviet masters. On the other hand he had money, a new car and the buzz of adventure. He was not complaining.

Chapter 8
The Headless Frogman

Harry was unaware that Roman was in fact the Second Secretary in the Russian Embassy, the senior KGB officer in England, called Vasili Duzhdev and answerable only to the Director of S Section of the KGB in Moscow. There were always potential dangers for someone in Roman's position making direct contact with a spy. His identity was almost certainly known to MI6 and their 'Watchers' tried to track him every time he left the Embassy compound. But he was well aware of this and found little difficulty in giving them the slip. For Roman personally the risks were slight. With diplomatic immunity the worst that could happen if he was caught on the wrong side of the law would be that he was flown home in disgrace. The risk was acceptable. He had to be careful though as he had no wish to compromise what was potentially his best source. He needed to measure Harry's reliability and this he chose to do personally. Each of the tasks that he set were in their way tests which Harry passed every time. Roman knew he was ready to be involved with more serious espionage. From now on his Russian contact could no longer be a 'legal' at the Embassy. It was time for an illegal resident to take over, someone unknown to MI5. The benefits in ease of contact were considerable, but so were the risks. An 'illegal' discovered in espionage would face a lengthy prison sentence.

Roman made his final visit to meet Harry in Weymouth in April 1956. Both of them were anxious to avoid Harry's contacts at work so he drove them in his new Renault for supper at the Crown Inn at Puncknowle, a small village ten miles from Weymouth. Unfortunately a work mate of Ethel's called Joan was there with a male friend. She recognized Harry and the couple came over to join them. After they had enjoyed a pint together the male friend, who had appeared on edge the whole time, excused himself and went to the lavatory. Joan apologised for his negative manner explaining that he was a member of the Royal Navy Shallow Diving Team who had been training for a special job in Portsmouth. He was very upset that after all their hard work the job had just been cancelled. To Roman this information was like a lightening strike. He knew that the Russian battleship *Ordzhonikidze* was about to visit Portsmouth with the soviet premier Nicolai Bulganin and party secretary Nikita Khrushchev on board. He could have a good guess what this special job might be. Harry was oblivious to the tension the conversation had generated but was forced to agree when Roman ordered him to drive straight back to Weymouth station from where he took the next train back to London.

Safely back in the Soviet Embassy Roman (or Duzhdev as he immediately became) contacted Moscow who gave him authorisation to investigate his suspicions. Two of his agents settled into lodgings in Portsmouth and it wasn't long before they successfully located two ex-navy frogmen, Buster Crabb and Bernard Smith registered under their own names in the Sally Port Hotel in Old Portsmouth. Lieutenant Commander Crabb had a distinguished war record and was already on the Russian register in the Lubyanka. The Soviet navy had serious suspicions that Crabb and his diving buddy Sydney Knowles the previous year had engaged in underwater spying on the Soviet cruiser *Sverdlov* also in Portsmouth harbour. It looked as if something similar might be planned for this visit. Duzhdev registered in a hotel near the Sally Port where he was able to keep a discreet eye on Crabb and Smith. Crabb looked unfit for underwater work. He was obviously overweight and was drinking heavily in the evenings. Smith, a much younger man, appeared to be sullen and unhappy. As soon as the *Ordzhonikidze* docked Duzhdev reported his suspicions to the captain. Bulganin and Khrushchev (or B and K as they were affectionately dubbed by the British press) were notified but were not unduly worried. Khrushchev asked to be kept informed.

As soon as B and K had left for London, Captain Igor Strelnikov took precautions to protect his ship. He ordered constant patrols below the hull by teams of soviet divers even fitting two wire jack-stays to run the length of the hull to ensure the divers were not swept away by the strong current in the harbour.

Around 11.00 p.m. on the night of April 19th two Russian divers arrested an unauthorised frogman who was trying to fix a device to the hull of the cruiser. Unfortunately in the struggle this unknown device fell to the seabed and was lost in the mud. Duzhdev was on board the *Ordzhonikidze* when the intruder was brought to the surface. On deck he was able to identify him as Commander Crabb. Whether because of his ill health, or over exertion in the struggle or his faulty breathing apparatus (which appeared very primitive to the Russians) Crabb collapsed and died.

Captain Strelnikov immediately informed the Russian Embassy in London and was instructed to follow whatever advice given to him by Duzhdev. As the ship was in no danger he decided that the matter was best dealt with quietly. The identity of the frogman was concealed and the body quietly disposed of in the sea.

The next evening Khrushchev in a speech he was making at a formal dinner, teased the British Prime Minister Anthony Eden about frogmen. Eden, who had specifically ordered the Admiralty not to investigate the *Ordzhonikidze*, was forced to make an abject apology in the Parliament. From their sources inside the Admiralty, the Russians learned that the British Navy wished to see if one of Russia's leading battleships was fitted with the latest underwater detection devices. Fourteen months later in June 1957 a headless body in a frogman's wetsuit was found in Chichester Harbour.

The Sussex coroner was unable to confirm the identity of the body, but he presumed it belonged to Commander Crabb. He also assumed the fact that the head, hands and feet were missing was due to natural marine rather than criminal activity. At the inquest Crabb's friend and previous diving buddy, Sydney Knowles showed the coroner a letter written by Buster Crabb the night before his fatal dive. For security reasons the existence of the letter was never made public.

Sally Port Hotel
Old Portsmouth
April 18th 1956

Dear Syd,

*You won't be entirely surprised but I've got myself
into a real ball-ache, and can't for the life of me see
how to get out of it. You know the little enterprise the
two of us undertook on the Sverdlov last year when
she visited Portsmouth; well I have been roped in for
something similar. The cruiser Ordzhonikidze, which
brought the two Russian nobs B and K on some sort
of State visit last week is anchored in Portsmouth
Harbour. The Admiralty badly wants further details
about its propellers as the O has been travelling
unexpectedly fast. What more they expected to learn
than we had already told them about the Sverdlov I
can't think.*

*Since their Lordships cut my towrope last year I was
in no way directly involved, but I knew all about it
from some of the lads in the navy diving team. They
were really excited about the operation.*

*Anyhow you know what the PM is like…one minute
'go', the next 'don't go' and so on. He finally pulled
the plug four weeks ago on the Navy's plan with a
very firm 'Niet.' The lads were really gutted. That is
where I come in. I am sure you know I have been
doing a whole mountain of nothing since being cast
ashore by the Navy, well I was approached by an
over-educated tosser called Nicholas Elliot who is*

one of the grand panjandrums of MI6 in London. I guess that the security services have suffered considerable loss of face over recent years and MI6 in particular with the defection of Burgess and McLean. Elliot thought a bit of frogman freelancing was what he called 'an acceptable risk' and in some convoluted way reckoned he could by-pass Eden's quite clear banning order. The spooks were looking for a coup de theatre to re-establish their reputation.

Because I had nothing else on, I said I would do it, and they gave me as diving buddy BS who you will remember from Gib. We did some combined training earlier in the week and a recce this am. The water was filthy and the bottom of the harbour full of shit ...you will remember this as it was much like our last trip. Unfortunately my gear wasn't working properly. I'm still using the equipment we took from the Ities in '42 and it is getting pretty worn. I had to surface in the harbour; fortunately well away from the target. BS started to panic and we cut the dive short and returned to the hotel. BS is adamant that he is not doing the job. He said I was too old and fat to be still diving (dammit I am only 55 though I must admit I am not as fit as I would like). He said I drank too much also. I lost my rag with him then and pointed out that I had been diving, and drinking, while he was still in nappies.

I know I shouldn't do this trip as a solo, but I feel I have committed myself even though the venture stinks like rotting fish. Actually I also need the money.

Tomorrow I shall go in with or without BS though I don't have a good feeling about it.

If things do go wrong the shit will hit the fan and I don't want my family to suffer. It's not Margaret. I know you didn't approve when we separated, but I don't have to worry about her, as she'll be OK. We were divorced last year and I heard she has another man in her life already! She won't get my naval pension because of the divorce. This should go to my mother Beatrice as next of kin. (I think you met her once and she is getting on a bit now.) I would have liked my fiancée/girl friend Pat Rose to get something also. I don't suppose you even know she exists as you and I haven't been in touch for some time. We have only just decided to get married and there is nothing official yet. Pat is the one who drove me down here but in true MI6 spying tradition I wasn't allowed to tell her what I was up to. If I snuff it I would like to think she was being looked after.

I am writing to you Syd for 'auld lang syne'. I know things haven't been OK between us recently, but from years of diving together I know you pretty well and I know I can depend on you to look after their interests. Anyhow there isn't anyone else I can ask. I wish you had been my buddy for tomorrow. I'm off to the bar for a quick bevvy before bed. With luck it'll drive away the glooms.

Yours in friendship

Buster.

Chapter 9
The Krogers

About the time in 1954 that Harry met George in Dulwich, Mr and Mrs Peter Kroger, a middle aged couple from New Zealand, moved into their new home. This was a bungalow, at No 45 Cranley Drive in Ruislip. Peter, an antiquarian bookseller, journeyed around Europe buying and selling books specializing in 19th century Americana and Victoriana. He was often to be seen at Sotheby's and Christie's where he soon built up a reputation as a cautious but responsible trader. His wife, Helen, joined the local WI and was known as Auntie Helen to the neighbour's children. To the FBI in America they were known as Lona and Morris Cohen and were wanted for espionage.

Morris was born in New York and aged 27 he joined the Spanish civil war as a foreign national volunteer. He was already a convinced communist and when he was injured in 1938 he returned to the USA and began serving soviet intelligence with the code name LUIS. In 1941 he married Lona Cohen (code name LESLE) who was also a communist and already an important link in the soviet spy chain. When Morris was drafted into the army in 1942 Lona continued to work for the Soviet Union holding together the *Volunteer Network* of spies. Her greatest contribution was carrying the secrets of the American atomic programme known as the Manhattan Project from Los Alamos to the Russian Consulate in New York. In 1948 Morris and Lona started to work for Colonel Rudolph Abel the Russian *rezident*, reactivating the *Volunteer* communications network in New York.

On 29th August 1949 the Russians carried out their first successful nuclear explosion to the consternation and mystification of the American Government. It became obvious then that secrets from the Manhattan Project based at Los Alamos had been given to the Soviets and the FBI started an intensive search for the spy or spies. By the summer of 1950 the Rosenberg Spy Ring was uncovered. Klaus Fuchs a British atomic scientist and David Greenglass an American soldier-machinist both worked at Los Alamos and confessed to betraying the secrets of the atomic bomb to the Russians. A further link in the chain, Morton Sobell, was arrested in Mexico and returned to the US to stand trial and Harry Gold with Julius and Ethel Rosenberg were arrested in New York on June 16th. Ethel Rosenberg was David Greenglass' sister. These arrests prompted an exodus from the US of many communist fellow travellers who were already feeling hounded by the oratory of Senator McCarthy. In August 1950 Morris and Lona Cohen, whose communist sympathies were well known to the FBI and whose house rent was paid by Julius Rosenberg, slipped quietly across the border into Mexico and out of sight of the American authorities. They were lucky to escape, as the FBI was close on their trail.

Julius and Ethel Rosenberg began their three-year ordeal in Sing Sing, which only ended when both were sent to the electric chair. Julius was the acknowledged leader of the *Volunteer* group but Ethel, though also a communist, knew nothing of the work. Her conviction and death remain a stain on the

American justice system. She was betrayed by her brother David, who provided the only evidence against her. It was the arrest of the Rosenbergs which prompted Morris and Lona, who had money and false passports ready prepared, to make a quick dash for Mexico and then a more leisurely journey via Spain and Czechoslovakia to Russia. There the KGB welcomed them.

For the next three and a half years both Cohens were trained in the Russian techniques of penetration. Lona specialised in photography and radio transmission and trained as a cypher clerk while Morris developed his background cover. Their next assignment was to be the communication hub for a new spy ring in England. Early in 1954 they made their way to Austria where they obtained passports from the New Zealand Embassy in the names of Kroger and so it was towards the end of 1954 Peter Kroger, bookseller, and his wife Helen both citizens of New Zealand arrived in England.

Chapter 10
The Positioning of Gordon Lonsdale

Throughout the 1950s the Royal Navy and the US Navy exchanged a great deal of sensitive information about submarine warfare. This was officially recognized in the Anglo American Mutual Defence Agreement of 1958. The Americans built the first nuclear submarine USS Nautilus (launched in 1954), which sailed from Honolulu in Hawaii to Britain under the North Pole arriving in Portland Harbour in August 1958. The US Navy shared with the Royal Navy the plans for their nuclear propulsion unit, which would be used in HMS Dreadnought Britain's first nuclear submarine, to be launched in 1960. In exchange the British shared with the Americans all their experimental results in underwater detection (known to the Americans as SONAR) and torpedo development.

Portland Harbour and the English Channel became a prime training site for realistic operational sea training, with tactical exercises engaging submerged submarines, not only for British and American navies, but for all NATO countries. The results of all the scientific research, sea trials, torpedo development and sonar counter mine detection systems were collated and recorded at the highly secret Admiralty Underwater Weapons Establishment on the Isle of Portland. It is not surprising that Portland became the key target for Russian espionage.

In March 1955 Gordon Lonsdale landed at Southampton docks from the liner SS America.

Lonsdale had standard Moscow instructions for an illegal. He was to spend whatever time was necessary building up an acceptable profile as a Canadian citizen that would stand intense scrutiny. The documentation he had acquired in Canada was flawless and up to the time of his arrest it was never questioned. His regular contact was by short wave radio directly from Moscow keeping any association with the London Embassy almost to nil. These flash messages in code were undetected and probably undetectable by British security and usually arrived between 3.00 and 4.00 in the morning. Through them Lonsdale was told what information his masters in the KGB required. Personal messages to his wife and all domestic and financial matters he communicated through Peter and Helen Kroger safe in their little house in Ruislip.

While staying in Toronto Lonsdale had decided to begin his stay in England studying at the London University School of Oriental and African studies. It was here ironically that many members of MI5 were sent for language courses. He was already fluent in four languages and used this time, not only to make useful contacts, but also to learn mandarin. During his first year he thoroughly embedded himself in English society. He was extremely sociable and never had any difficulty in making friends, particularly girl friends, who described him as charming, cheerful and full of fun. At least twice a year he took his holidays in one of the Eastern European countries (usually Czechoslovakia) where the KGB arranged for him to meet up with his wife Galina. For three years in England he had a strong relationship with an Italian girl called Carla Panizzi but when his son was born in Russia in the summer of 1958 he felt a greater responsibility to his wife and child and broke with Carla encouraging her to return to San Remo. After Carla he made do with frequent casual relationships mainly with lonely girls from Yugoslavia and Poland. Galina did not approve of these affairs, which she guessed at, but as long as he didn't tell her about them she accepted that they were a necessary part of his cover story. Besides she knew she had his heart now and for always.

Soon after his arrival in London Lonsdale had rented a flat in The White House in Albany Street near Regent's Park. This was comfortable but not luxurious and paid for with money he received from Moscow via Switzerland. In 1957, with some English friends, he founded the Automatic Merchandising Company and the Thanet Trading Company. He had made it his business to learn about trading machines while living in New York and reckoned there was a good future for them in England. Through these companies he sold and rented jukeboxes and bubble-gum vending machines to pubs and cafes. He also had what on the outside appeared to be quite a lucrative business in leasing fruit machines to pubs. These became known locally as one-arm bandits. Moscow initially financed these enterprises. The work didn't inspire Lonsdale at all but it did give him an excellent cover story, a reason why he was in England, and an excuse for travelling widely in the southern counties. None of these companies made much of a profit. He was not a very good capitalist.

Lonsdale considered himself both a patriot and a soldier for peace. In America, and also to a lesser extent in Great Britain, after the end of the Second World War there were powerful elements in government who seriously promoted the idea of a pre-emptive strike against the Soviet Union. The work for the Russian government of the British scientist Dr Klaus Fuchs and the penetration of Los Alamos nuclear laboratory in New Mexico had given the soviets the technology they needed to produce their own nuclear weapons and to ensure an uneasy balance of atomic power. Lonsdale's work was to carry on this information gathering in particular to collect as much information as he could about the naval strength of America and Great Britain, as their nuclear submarines were the most likely delivery systems for NATO atomic weapons. This information gathering was greatly facilitated by the US-UK Mutual Defence Agreement of 1958, which established the exchange of classified information on nuclear weapons between the two countries. The agreement ensured that most of the US nuclear secrets were available to the British Admiralty. A particular interest of the soviets was to discover the allies' secrets of underwater submarine detection and anything they could about their nuclear submarine programme. Vickers in Barrow in Furness was at this time building Dreadnought, Britain's first nuclear submarine, to American specifications with an American nuclear propulsion plant. This became one of Lonsdale's primary targets. The Russians believed the more relaxed British security would provide an admirable backdoor to American nuclear secrets.

Lonsdale concocted a secondary cover story that he was gathering information about rogue German Scientists working on germ warfare at the Chemical Defence Experimental Establishment at Porton Down. In his role as peacemaker he could justify his actions as helping to prevent a future holocaust to any British idealists who might detect his activities. He was also clear that any spilling of nuclear secrets by the British would help continue to weaken the US-UK alliance which had already been shaken by the recent betrayals of Burgess, McLean and Philby.

When the KGB gave Harry Houghton's name to Lonsdale they let him know that Harry was already thoroughly compromised by the Polish UB and earlier KGB contacts. By this time Lonsdale had built up a small but effective network gathering useful information, but Moscow's instructions were quite clear. Houghton was to be the top priority. First contact was by phone with the tried and tested method, a message from a fictitious friend in Warsaw. He arranged to meet Harry at the caravan on Portland.

Harry never swallowed the story of the Warsaw friend, which by now was pretty thin and overused, but Lonsdale quickly worked out that Houghton was a vain and shifty man who would do whatever was required for a little money. As Moscow had indicated he was by now thoroughly hooked. Lonsdale played him like an experienced angler. He guessed Harry enjoyed the thrill of spying. It gave him a sense of importance and he thought he could get away with everything. There were moments of tension between them but Lonsdale was skilfully able to reassure Houghton. Harry had been providing some adequate information for three years and though Lonsdale never trusted him, by flattery, bribery and veiled threats he found he could get him to do whatever he wanted. It was time for Harry to deliver. Though he continued to protest that he had no access to secret information, Lonsdale pointed out to him forcibly that his girlfriend Ethel did.

Chapter 11
Pawn Sacrifice

From the moment Harry first kissed Ethel she was never really in control of her own destiny. Their relationship developed at a slow pace, something both of them were happy with. They were regulars at the Elm Tree in Langton Herring and the small table in the snug became their special place. Ethel was upset if they found other customers sitting in their corner. Though she had little sense of style she always made an effort when the two of them went out together. Frequently Harry would compliment her on her dress or appearance. She enjoyed their drives around North Dorset in his new car and the supper of scampi and chips in a pub somewhere, which rounded off the day. Ethel was concerned that Harry drank too much, but he never seemed to be the worse for wear so eventually she stopped worrying. Occasionally she even had a second glass of wine herself.

When Ethel was promoted from Stores to the Drawing Office (Records Section) they went out to the Elm Tree to celebrate her new job and increased pay. Harry insisted on buying a round of drinks for all the regulars and when they had settled back in their corner he told her that he was divorcing Peggy, that it was her he loved and would like them to be married. When he dropped her outside her parent's house he kissed her...the first time she had been kissed for 30 years. For some weeks Ethel had been desperately hoping that their relationship would develop from the platonic friendship of the last year.

At 41 she didn't feel too old to marry and if he asked she would say 'yes.' At least this would spite Uncle John. When, once again, their weekend expedition was cancelled at short notice she couldn't hide her upset. In a burst of anxiety she questioned him about his sudden trips to London, but he promised her there wasn't another girl. She wanted so much to believe him. She asked around the office and though Sheila confessed to being fond of Harry and thinking him handsome, she assured Ethel there was nothing between them. It was Ethel who was known at the UWE as Harry's girl.

'I've got to go to London again this week-end,' he told her just before Christmas and Ethel couldn't hide her distress and started to weep. 'Don't cry Old Girl.' He clumsily tried to comfort her. 'You can come with me if you like. We can do a show or something if that's what you want.' It was exactly what Ethel wanted. She dried her eyes, bursting with happiness.

They took the train from Weymouth on Friday evening. Because he was ex-Navy Harry was entitled to be a member of the Victory Services Club near Marble Arch. 'This is where I always stay when I come to London,' he told her. It really was a gloomy old-fashioned sort of place, which Ethel found a little intimidating.

'What do I do when we get inside?' she whispered.

'You'll have to sign an application form,' he told her. 'Don't worry its just a formality. They'll know you're not really my wife. Most of the couples here are on a one night stand and no-one really cares if we're married or not.' She filled in the form and signed her name as Mrs Harry Houghton.

While she was writing she felt that everyone's eyes were staring at her. 'See, no-one's worried,' Harry murmured. It all felt rather sordid to Ethel but the man behind the desk didn't blink an eye so she tried to be unconcerned. *I wish I really was Mrs Harry Houghton,* she thought. He had told her on many occasions that when his divorce was finalised they ought to get married, but she knew it wouldn't be easy for her to abandon her mother, Aunt Angela and Uncle John. That night when she went to sleep in Harry's arms she had never been happier.

On Saturday morning Harry busied himself on the phone. As promised he succeeded in booking tickets for the matinee of the musical *Salad Days* at the Adelphi Theatre. Ethel shone with happiness as she anticipated a morning looking around London with her man. Harry knowing his next bit of news wouldn't go down so well looked uncomfortable as they drank a cup of coffee before setting off. 'I've just had a call from the chap I'm supposed to meet. I've arranged a lunch date. Sorry, Old Girl. Hope it won't spoil the weekend.' Ethel's face fell. 'It's not a woman honestly. It's an American officer I sometimes do business with. He said he'd like to meet you, so I've booked a table for the three of us in a restaurant near the theatre.'

The friend was Gordon Lonsdale who introduced himself to Ethel as Commander Alex Johnson of the US Navy. Lonsdale held her hand just a fraction too long. 'Call me Alex,' he told her with a friendly grin. 'I don't like to use my rank unless I'm on official business.' Harry, presumably, was comfortable with this lie and Ethel was completely charmed by Alex. Over lunch the talk turned to ballet, which was one of Ethel's secret passions. 'The Bolshoi are coming to London in the New Year,' Alex announced. 'I've a friend at the Embassy, that is the American Embassy, who can get tickets for the three of us if you'd like.' Ethel shivered with excitement. This was turning out to be the best weekend of her life.

Alex showed considerable interest in the UWE. As he explained to her, 'a major part of my job is to check how well you limeys look after all the secrets entrusted to you by our navy.' Ethel knew all about this. With the recent Mutual Defence Agreement, more and more information and data from the US had been pouring through her office. 'Just at the moment my Admiral wants to know if your Navy is managing to keep secret everything about nuclear submarines. Your nuclear submarine Dreadnought has an American power unit, you know, and we wouldn't want anyone else getting hold of any of our secrets.'

'Though I've heard about the sub…we call it *The Black Death*… there's nothing really I can say,' she told him. 'Portland won't have anything to do with it until sea trials. Honestly, Vickers at Barrow are tight as a Scotsman's sporran,' Alex was so easy to talk to Ethel chattered away explaining that most of her job was routine and boring, filing pamphlets about the tests on submarine warfare and sending description of various machine parts to different firms all over the country. 'Last week,' she told him, 'there was a really horrid letter from the Navy Torpedo Factory complaining we hadn't sent them the latest spec for the Mark XII. Mrs Strange, our office supervisor had been really rough with us even though she knew that with Mary Fisher off sick Pamela and I have to do all the filing.' Alex was very sympathetic.

Ethel dipped into her handbag and produced a scrap of paper on which she had written all the numbers of those pamphlets she had to collect and collate. 'That was just yesterday's lot. This is all my job is collecting files, requesting parts and forwarding information. Really quite boring.'

When it was time for Harry and Ethel to go to the theatre, Alex insisted on paying for lunch. He helped her on with her coat and put his hand on her arm. 'Don't downplay the importance of your work Ethel. If it really is just routine and wasn't vital to British and American defence, would I have been sent over from America to check up on it?'

Ethel shyly asked Alex if he could call her Bunty as Harry did. She explained that she never really liked the name Ethel, which was horribly dated and anyhow all those close to her called her Bunty. Alex laughingly agreed and asked where the nickname came from. 'I was a fat little thing as a child, and it sort of stuck.'

'Well you have a handsome figure now Bunty,' Alex assured her. Harry nodded his agreement and she felt good about herself.

The weekend after the London trip Bunty helped Harry decorate the cottage he'd rented in Broadwey. She had a real flair for colour and enjoyed choosing the paints for his bedroom and sitting room.

She even agreed to sew the curtains and sewing was something she hated. She was relieved that he was no longer in the poky caravan and she had a secret thrill in helping him smarten up his home.

In the New Year, as he had promised, Alex arranged to treat Harry and Bunty to the ballet. The Bolshoi were performing *Spartacus* at the Albert Hall. Bunty was proud to be sitting between two such handsome men in seats that must have cost a fortune. Alex whispered that it was the first time this ballet had been danced outside Moscow. 'The Bolshoi are only in England for a few more days and it'll probably be years before they come back again.' Bunty loved the music by Khatchaturian. Alexander Begak danced Spartacus and Lydia Ushakova was his wife Phrygia. It was electric when they danced the pas de deux together, so beautiful, but also sad. She cried with Phrygia when they killed Spartacus and the slaves carried off his body. Alex lent her his hankie, which she used and then stuffed into her coat pocket.

At the end of the evening Alex insisted on walking back to the Club with the two of them. 'Could you possibly get hold of two pamphlets for me, one on homing torpedoes, and another on those devices that are towed behind warships to confuse the enemy.' He held her hand. 'Please see if you can help me. Also I would be grateful for anything on ASDIC.' Bunty knew that ASDIC was nothing to do with the Americans and fleetingly wondered why he needed this information. However she felt so good about herself and the world that she readily agreed.

'I can arrange to get the material to Alex,' Harry assured her.

Chapter 12
The Portland Spy Ring

Admiralty secrets began to flow from the UWE at Portland to Moscow in a torrent. Lonsdale would let Harry know what information he required. Harry would tell Bunty which files to look for and she would take advantage of the lax security during the lunch interval to collect the booklets from the cabinets. She would slip these into one of the white Admiralty envelopes and at the end of work she would walk with them through the main gate. On these occasions Harry would pick her up by car and drop the files off at his cottage. That evening Harry would photograph the documents with the Minox camera Nikki had given him and taught him to use. Next morning at the Broadwey post office he would send the film to a PO box in London. Helen Kroger provided the next link in the chain. She had been trained by Moscow in the intricacies of espionage photography and communication. Diagrams and data she would convert into microdots, text she would encode and send to Moscow by short wave radio.

When Peter and Helen Kroger had first moved into Cranley Drive the rep who insured Peter's antique books had advised them to fit more secure locks on the house. This they had enthusiastically done, at the same time converting the bathroom to a photographic darkroom and building a hidden storage compartment in the basement and adapting the attic space for a powerful short wave radio. Together they had installed a 74 foot internal aerial, which ensured excellent reception. When Helen had processed the microdots, Peter Kroger would conceal them in carefully selected antique books and then travel abroad to pass these on to one of his agents for transmission to Moscow. He would use the foreign trip to bring more cash back into England, which helped lubricate the whole network. So much information was flowing from the UWE that Peter and Helen were hard pressed to process it all. Under such urgent pressure Lonsdale was aware that SHAH and ASYA, code names for Harry and Bunty, were desparately weak links in his security. By 1960 Harry was drinking heavily. Lonsdale, still calling himself Alex, was finding it increasingly difficult to maintain the pretence to Bunty that he was a serving American officer. He suspected that she might have guessed the truth, but chose not to face it. True to their training the Krogers had never met Harry or Bunty though they were obviously aware of their existences. Harry, however, had no idea where the information went after he had posted it.

By the beginning of 1959 certain officers in MI5 were growing increasingly alarmed about the possibility of soviet penetration particularly in the security services themselves. Confidence had been fragile since two senior officers Guy Burgess and Donald McLean had run off to Moscow to protect Kim Philby and then he in turn successfully slipped away from Beirut. Philby was actually head of British Intelligence in Washington while actively serving the KGB, a terrible blow to morale. There were strong suspicions that Anthony Blunt, the de facto recruiting officer for the Cambridge spies, had for years been working for the soviet government and MI5 at the same time, but he was off limits as he had the protection of Buckingham Palace.

Years later the Director of MI5 put Peter Wright, the agency's scientific officer in charge of a working party they called FLUENCY. The brief for his committee was to examine all unsolved allegations about soviet penetration of the services. FLUENCY began to uncover a raft of evidence. Peter Wright commented to colleagues that the KGB must have known more about the business of MI5 and 6 than our own Home Secretary.

When Wright reported his initial findings to the Director, Roger Hollis, he was told none of his evidence would be sufficient for a prosecution. Unless suspects confessed there wasn't much the law officers could do about it. Wright was told the best option was to get them to confess under a promise of immunity from prosecution. With this promise MI6 'inquisitors' would attempt under gentle interrogation to squeeze out more names or to turn them. The services were already so full of double and triple agents that it was often impossible to work out who was giving useful information to whom. Sometimes, Wright thought, it would be easier to suggest to his opposite number in Moscow that they just exchange a list of names. Unsurprisingly ever since he was given the FLUENCY job Peter Wright became the most unpopular officer in MI5 surrounded as he was by a miasma of suspicions and doubts. Few colleagues wanted to speak to him in case they were the next to be fingered. For some time the relationship between the CIA and the British Secret Service had been extremely fragile. The CIA complained that The

Service was as leaky as a sieve and refused co-operation. Roger Hollis the enigmatic DG of MI5 and the sanctimonious James Jesus Angleton, long-serving head of US counter intelligence, were barely on speaking terms.

Given the longstanding tensions between the two countries, it is ironic that it was evidence from the CIA that gave MI5 their greatest coup. In April 1959 information came to James Angleton from a new source in Poland. The CIA called their source *Sniper* and for once, Angleton was prepared to share his information with what he called 'You Brits'. The code name for *Sniper* in MI5 officially was *Lavinia*. The name must have been chosen by some back-office boffin with a classical education as in Book 7 of the Aeneid, Lavinia's hair catches fire apparently an omen predicting a world war. It was all rather pretentious so around the office the source was still usually referred to as *Sniper*. From the first material passed on to MI5 they could only guess that he was a Polish officer partly because of the poor quality of his spoken German and partly the excellent quality of his material. He informed the CIA about 'two spies one in British intelligence and one in the Royal Navy.' He called them *Lambda 1* and *Lambda 2*.

Angleton certainly enjoyed telling Peter Wright it appeared his department had been penetrated, probably because he was still embarrassed by his friendship with Philby while Kim had been working in Washington. 'Tell that stuck up prick Hollis that his service is as full of holes as a colander,' he told him smugly. *Sniper* had seen three secret documents about the latest MI5 scientific research, which he accurately described. It was Wright's job to find out how the KGB had got hold of these. He eventually concluded that *Lambda 1* did not exist and the documents *Sniper* had seen had been stolen from an Embassy safe in Brussels two years earlier. Wright informed the Americans about this. It was not until the following year that the truth emerged that *Lambda 1* was actually an MI6 officer called George Blake who at the time was stationed in Berlin. For ideological reasons, between 1955 -1961 Blake betrayed the names of over 40 agents to the Russians. When brought to justice, at his trial he was sentenced to 42 year in prison. However after only four years in jail he managed to escape over the wall of Wormwood Scrubs eventually being smuggled into Easy Germans in the back of a camper van. Blake was one of the few British spies who was not public school, homosexual or both. Wright was unable to find out who *Lambda 2* was.

In March 1960 *Sniper* was able to identify *Lambda 2* as a spy working for Naval Intelligence with a name that sounded like 'Huiton.' It was not difficult then to identify *Lambda 2* as Harry Houghton now working for the secret Underwater Weapons Establishment at Portland in Dorset. How embarrassing it was for MI5 to discover that Houghton was already on the Agency registry of suspects but had been cleared five years earlier. Even a superficial search showed that he led a lifestyle well beyond his pay scale. That ten years earlier he had worked for the naval attaché in the embassy in Warsaw clinched it. Houghton was the spy now it was necessary to collect the evidence to prove it.

More important MI5 also needed to uncover his contacts. A team of watchers was assembled to follow Houghton and in July he was seen to meet a man in Waterloo Road and exchange packages with him. The man drove a white Studebaker, which records showed was registered to a Canadian citizen called Gordon Lonsdale. MI5 gave Lonsdale the code name *Last Act.*

MI5 quickly discovered that Lonsdale was a businessman who traded in jukeboxes and bubble-gum machines. He led the life of a playboy and seemed to have plenty of money. Unofficially the spooks were able to bug his flat in Albany Street and his office in Wardour Street. Houghton met with Lonsdale again in August. The Watchers from the security service were able to establish a presence in a café near the Old Vic before the meeting. They saw packages being exchanged again and were fortunate to overhear Lonsdale tell Harry that he would be abroad till early October. Later that afternoon the Watchers followed him to the Midland Bank where he deposited a suitcase and a parcel wrapped in brown paper.

After carefully applied pressure on the Directors of Midland Bank by Roger Hollis, MI5 were given permission to open Lonsdale's deposit box. This they did on September 5th. Wright and the other officers involved realised at once they had hit the jackpot. Besides the suitcase and parcel there was a miniature camera called a Praktika, ideal for photographing documents and a second camera – a Minox. There was also a Ronson cigarette lighter which later x-ray revealed had a secret compartment in the base. In this compartment was a one-time pad, an essential piece of equipment for a spy to send messages in code. Lonsdale was no casual cutout or contact but a full-blown illegal resident and KGB agent. The suitcase was taken from the bank on 17th September to the MI5 laboratory near St Pauls. There the contents including the one-time pad were carefully copied, the film in the Minox developed and then everything returned to the deposit box in the bank. The developed film showed pictures of Lonsdale and a smiling woman together in a city abroad, which someone in the office identified as Prague. There were general congratulations by everyone involved at this brilliant and successful counter-espionage coup. Everything turned sour when one of the radio operators monitoring all the routine radio traffic from the Russian Embassy produced a print-out of recent radio activity. After long periods of silence in transmissions there had been a burst of receiver messages on 6th and 18th of September. Despite being unable to decode these, the inference from their dates was clear. Both dates coincided exactly with MI5's Midland Bank operation. It appeared to Peter Wright that despite all the care he had taken the Russians now knew that Lonsdale was blown. All those involved at MI5 feared he had left the country and, like Burgess, McLean and Philby, he had been tipped off and would not be returning.

Chapter 13
Red Gambit – Knight Sacrifice

The corridors were ominously quiet. Lonsdale had been in the Lubyanka building in Moscow only once before over five years earlier. He had expected a welcoming reception desk and smiling assistance accompanied by the hum of a vast anthill of animated workers selling their souls to the state. Instead all he could see were long marble corridors and heavy wooden doors firmly closed. He looked round uncertain what to do next. A bell rang behind him and the metal gates of the old fashioned lift opened. A young KGB captain came up to him and saluted. 'Major Molody? The General is waiting for you. Please follow me.' They entered the lift together. Lonsdale tried to find out why there was so little activity in the building but the young captain maintained a stony silence. When the lift stopped the captain gestured Lonsdale down the corridor. 'The General is in the room at the end of the corridor on your left.' The gates closed behind him. Waiting was General Aleksandr Sakharovsky, Director of the First Chief Directorate of the Committee for State Security effectively the head of the KGB.

Lonsdale stood for a moment outside the famous door on the third floor of the Lubyanka, headquarters of the KGB, trying to compose himself. After all from this room Lavrenti Beria in his 15 years as head of the NKVD had sent hundreds of thousands of people to their death or the Gulags during the bloody period of the purges. Now Moscow had sent for him and he didn't know why. He steadied his breathing, straightened his suit. There hadn't been time to get into uniform and this fretted him. He knocked on the door.

General Sakharovsky was sitting behind a vast walnut desk covered with stacks of papers. He looked up and for a moment, studying Lonsdale through his gold-framed spectacles, then beckoned Lonsdale forward. 'Major Konon Molody reporting as ordered Sir.' Lonsdale saluted.

'Come in Molody. Come and sit.' He waved Lonsdale towards a chair. 'I don't think we have met before.' He didn't wait for a response. 'You were assigned by my predecessor Panyushkin I believe.'

'Yes Sir.' Lonsdale tried to stop his voice squeaking. Now was not the time to show any weakness.

'You received my message?'

'Yes Sir. It was passed to me a week ago. Control said it was urgent. I came as quickly as I could.'

'How are Lona and Morris or the Krogers I believe I should now call them?' Before Lonsdale could answer Sakharovsky continued. 'You have seen your wife and children?'

'No Sir. I came straight here. I haven't seen Galina since Prague. The baby I have yet to meet.'

Sakharovsky picked up a sheet of paper from a pile on the corner of his desk. 'I have reason to believe that British Intelligence may know of your existence. They are also on to SHAH. I am told both of you are under close observation.'

'I have been most careful sir. I have constructed my identity as Lonsdale over many years.

I feel certain I would have noticed if I had been discovered.'

'However certain you may feel,' the General glanced down again at his piece of paper, 'I have reliable information that British Military Intelligence have your flat under surveillance. Given the unreliability of SHAH, which I know you have always recognized, this is not altogether surprising.'

Is this a reprimand, Lonsdale wondered? *Bloody Houghton will be the death of me.*

Sakharovsky again referred to the sheet of paper on his desk. There was a long pause as he read on. 'The reports I have of your operation are excellent.' Lonsdale started to relax. This sounded like a reprieve. 'You seem to have led a very full, perhaps I should say fulfilling social life.'

Lonsdale squirming inside his jacket tried to keep his face impassive. Fleetingly he thought of the many sexual encounters he had enjoyed in his role as playboy jukebox seller. Usually the KGB did not object to this sort of activity. After all it was part of his cover. He remained silent as Sakharovsky continued to read the paper.

'Yes some very good work in England,' Lonsdale relaxed a little. 'Five years is a long time for an illegal.'

'As my identity is now known, I am grateful to you for bringing me out in time sir. I hope I will be able to continue to serve the Motherland for many more years in some other country.' Lonsdale thought his continuous years on active service had earned him the right to make one request. 'May I ask if I could I see my wife and my new son before I am reassigned?'

'Yes, yes.' Sakharovsky acknowledged the request with a wave of the hand and levered himself from his chair. Lonsdale immediately stood up. He was surprised how small the general was. But then Napoleon Bonaparte was only five foot five inches tall and he had heard that Joseph Stalin was only five foot six inches. Lack of height obviously did not equate with lack of power. The general studied him in silence and then beckoned him over to the window.

He gestured over the Lubyanka Square below. 'Iron Felix.' Lonsdale looked at the vast statue of Felix Dzerzhinsky the first head of the Cheka. It was newly sculpted. Lonsdale had heard stories about this monstrosity but never before seen it. 'Fifteen tons of iron.' The General paused and seemed to Lonsdale for a moment uncertain how to continue. 'I met Felix once; well not exactly met. I was a cadet officer in the Cheka and was summoned to this building for a briefing shortly before Felix died. He was a terrible man who did terrible things for the Revolution, but I am told he loved his wife and son. It was he who set the standards for the Cheka, which were continued in the NKVD and now in our KGB. Officers were always expected to give total obedience to their superiors and to put the needs of the Rodina – our beloved Motherland – before their own.' He continued to gaze out of the window as the evening sunlight now slanting across the square left the giant statue in shadow. 'You have earned the right for a more gentle assignment and for time to spend with your wife and children, but your country has need of you once again and this is something only you can do. I would like you to return to England and continue your work. This is not an order but a request from me. You and SHAH, I expect, will shortly be arrested. Even the English cannot go on missing clues forever. Because you are an illegal you cannot expect to be expelled, as a diplomat would be. For you it will be trial and prison. But we will arrange an exchange for you as soon as possible. That is my assurance to you.'

A black cloud wrapped itself round Lonsdale's brain and he felt his stomach begin to knot. It did not seem to him that he had a great deal of option. A request from General Sakharovsky was not significantly different from a written order. He quickly decided that if he was to have any future the answer had to be yes. 'I will be honoured to have the chance to serve the Motherland in whatever way I can.' He was quietly proud of the confidence in his voice. 'Is it permitted to know why I am to do this sir?'

'I regret Major that I cannot tell you any more. You are not even to try and guess. You will carry on your life exactly as you would if this conversation had not happened. Not too much of a hardship I think.' He barked a short laugh. 'At your trial you will tell them nothing. Nothing that would give them any understanding about how we work. Do not be too tidy. You must leave sufficient clues to guarantee that even the English can prove you are a spy.'

'What about the Krogers sir?'

'They are currently abroad, but when they return to England they must take their chance.' He glanced down at the sheet of paper he still held. 'I believe they are as yet undetected. On no account are you to let them know that your identity has been discovered. I expect SHAH will go to prison for a long time and ASYA is likely to be collateral damage.'

'That is no particular loss sir. I was told his information has never been more than confirmation of what we already know.'

'He is more important than you could possibly realise Major. The whole of your operation is vital to Russia.' He handed Lonsdale a blue travel pass which he noticed had already been filled in. 'Now you must have some leave. Go and stay with your wife and children. Return to London by the middle of October. I will see you again when your assignment is finished.'

Chapter 14
Sir Roger Hollis

Roger Hollis was a very secretive man. Perhaps this is no bad thing for someone who was Director General of MI5 for nearly ten years and had worked for the Security Service for most of his adult life. Few in the Service knew anything about his history or his present social life. He was rumoured to have a wife and a young son at Eton or was it by now Cambridge University, but no one in the office had met them. Peter Wright echoed the thoughts of most of his colleagues when he expressed his dislike of his boss and doubted his ability. 'Hollis was never a popular figure in the office. He was a dour, uninspiring man with an off-putting authoritarian manner. I must confess I never liked him. But even those who were well disposed doubted his suitability for the top job.' Some were convinced that Hollis was carrying on an affair with his secretary, as she stayed working with him much longer than was appropriate for someone of her seniority. Others believed the secretary, Val Hammond, was a clandestine lesbian in love with a Russian-speaking agent called Natalia and that Hollis protected both of them. At the time when Ian Fleming was enthralling the public with the activities of James Bond, anything was possible.

Hollis had not always been a dull fish. As a classical scholar at Worcester College Oxford in the twenties he had thrown himself into the social life of the university. Evelyn Waugh described him as 'a good bottle man' and his many left wing friends may or may not have met with the approval of his father, the Bishop of Taunton. Because he spent more time at parties and the university chess club than the libraries he left Oxford without a degree. Despite this he soon found a job working as a journalist in Hong Kong and then moved on to China working for the British American Tobacco Company for the next eight years. During this time he made friends with Agnes Smedley a well-known left wing journalist whose lover was Richard Sorge perhaps the most effective Russian spy of the twentieth century. How deeply Hollis absorbed Sorge's ideas is unknown, but when tuberculosis forced him to leave China he returned to England via Russia and immediately made attempts to join the British Secret Service.

Hollis was not put off by initial rejections and eventually Jane Sissmore, a casual tennis partner who was also responsible for overseeing all Soviet operations in Britain, persuaded MI5 to take him on as her assistant. In 1940 she was sacked and Hollis took her place as head of F Division, by 1953 he was Deputy Director General of MI5 and by 1956 he succeeded Dick White as the Director General. His rapid rise through the organization was without ever any serious security clearance.

There is no evidence to link Hollis directly to the numerous security disasters while he was at the top of the British agency whose purpose was to root out soviet spies, but Peter Wright and others were confused by his apparent indifference to the discovery of the Portland spy ring. It was not till his retirement in 1965 and the further evidence of Soviet penetration with the efforts of George Blake and John Vassal that the FLUENCY Committee began to wonder if Hollis might not be the best fit for the agent codenamed *Elli* first identified by the Russian cipher clerk Igor Gouzenko who defected to the Canadians in 1945. Could the Director of MI5 have been a Soviet agent for nearly thirty years?

Chapter 15
Last Act

The atmosphere in the control room at MI5 was akin to panic. Peter Wright kept pestering his team of Watchers to make certain that Lonsdale had not returned unnoticed. He made such a fuss that Roger Hollis the Director General summoned him. When he entered the DG's office Wright found Hollis hunched over a chessboard, the pieces spread widely. Hollis waved him to the chair conveniently placed as if ready for an opponent. 'Do you play Peter?' he asked.

'I do Sir, but not very well,' Wright answered.

'You should work at it', Hollis told him. 'It's the greatest war game ever invented. This game,' he pointed at the board, 'is the sixth game of the world championship played last summer, when Mikhail Tal claimed the crown from Botvinnik. Tal's only 24 years old. My son showed it to me. Adrian's already won two chess blues for Cambridge University and is playing first board this year.'

Peter Wright had never seen the DG so animated, and the pride he showed in his son's achievement was obvious, surprising and very human.

'Botvinnik is playing white, here let me show you.' He rearranged the pieces back to their starting positions. 'The Champion makes the conventional opening move of King's pawn to d4. Tal counters this by moving his knight to f6, the classic King's Indian Defence. He now allows Botvinnik to advance his pawns until white appears to control the centre.' Hollis was totally absorbed in his game to the exclusion of everything else. Peter Wright watched him fascinated. 'Now Botvinnik moves his bishop to g2. This is called the Fianchetto Variation. It appears that there is no way black's plan of attack can succeed as white's kingside is more solidly defended. But that does not take into account the brilliance of Tal. Watch what happened.' Hollis moved the pieces around the board so quickly that there was no way Wright could follow. 'Tal sacrifices his knight and starts a complicated tactical melee which takes Botvinnik by surprise. Tal loves confusion. The world champion is not able to find a good defence in the given time.' He tipped over the white king. 'Game and ultimately match to the young pretender. A triumph for nerve and timing, don't you see? It was the unexpected surrender of the black knight, which threw Botvinnik's cautious plan into disarray.

Hollis leaned back in his chair and shook his head as if to shake the chess pieces from his mind. 'Anyhow about your current concerns Peter, you worry too much. I personally see no reason to think that Lonsdale will not return. Your operation has been as careful and thoroughly conducted as is possible and I do congratulate you. If however Lonsdale does fail to return we will then have to assume that there has been a leak somewhere. That is something that will have to be thoroughly investigated, however I am confident it will not come to that.'

The DG's calmness went some way to pacify Wright, but the last two weeks in September and first two in October was a difficult time for him and his team. On 1st October Harry Houghton made a routine visit to London but met no one. Then on 17th October one of the Watchers spotted Lonsdale entering his office in Wardour Street. MI5 were aware that to follow an experienced operative like Lonsdale without the tracker being spotted was extremely unlikely. It took two weeks of careful shuffling and changing of personnel before he was seen to enter 45 Cranley Drive in Ruislip.

The neighbours identified the occupants of No 45 as a charming New Zealand couple called Kroger, who were currently on holiday abroad. Helen Kroger had told them that a friend would be house-sitting while they were away, but to expect them back in at the beginning of November.

When the Krogers returned to their house Lonsdale moved back to his flat. Though he immediately started up his nightly radio contacts, the boffins at GCHQ were concerned that they were no longer able to decode the radio messages to Moscow that they were intercepting. Hollis approved Peter Wright's request to break into his flat and this was done on a day Lonsdale went to Suffolk on jukebox business. A quick check on the one-time pads hidden in the Ronson showed that he was still using the same codes. Most of the messages were about SHAH who Wright realised must be Houghton. There was a stream of instructions from Moscow as to which files Lonsdale was to get hold of and a sad message from his wife in Russia saying how much she missed him and wanted him home. *It will be some time before you get home my lad*, Wright thought.

The Admiralty, who had been fully briefed about Houghton's activities, agreed to let him run for three more months in the hope that further members of

Lonsdale's network could be identified, but on New Year's Day 1961 the CIA informed MI5 that *Sniper* was demanding that America honour their promise and grant him political asylum. *Sniper* turned out to be a disaffected Polish intelligence officer called Michael Goleniewski. It was his information that first alerted MI5 to the identity of *Lambda 2* and the Americans who were proud of their potential defector did not feel they could delay his lifting any longer. It was some years later that questions began to be asked about *Sniper's* trustworthiness. Could he be a triple agent, a plant by the KGB whose carefully selected secrets would help to cover up a high-level asset at the heart of British Security? Was the whole Portland operation a complicated KGB intrigue to sow further distrust between the British and American intelligence services and their respective navies. At the time *Sniper's* defection was seen as a triumph. Two years later Goleniewski's information was never full trusted.

The spycatchers could not afford to wait any longer. When *Sniper* was safely in American hands, the Russians would know that Lonsdale's and Houghton's covers were blown. It was time for MI5 to bring in the police.

Chapter 16
End Game

None of his colleagues in Special Branch liked Detective Superintendent George Smith or even admired him, certainly not as much as he admired himself. It is the Special Branch of the Metropolitan Police, which has responsibility for counter terrorism and other actions against the state. The Deputy Commissioner of the Met certainly had little time for George Smith's overweening self promotion and arrogance, but as a senior officer in Special Branch Smith was the only real choice to oversee this operation. The Deputy Commissioner of MI5 handed him the file with a caution. 'Don't mess this up George. It's destined for the front pages.' The file contained the summary of evidence against five individuals; two English who lived in Weymouth, a Canadian called Lonsdale and two New Zealanders who lived in London all of whom appeared to be engaged in espionage. Smith knew that MI5 and MI6 were permitted by special order to undertake surveillance and collect evidence, but historically they were not allowed to make arrests. That was the prerogative of the police, and in this case the Special Branch.

The contact officer between the security service and Special Branch was Peter Wright. George Smith had little time for Wright, mentally dismissing him as some sort of second division boffin, a technical expert specialising in radio intercepts. Wright took Smith through the evidence, which provided a strong prima facie case for a charge of espionage and emphasised the need for speed. 'If we don't arrest them at once,' Wright stressed, 'Lonsdale and the Krogers are certain to scarper. The CIA have told us *Sniper* will defect and seek asylum sometime this week. The Russians will know and we'll lose them.

George Smith was at his most pompous. 'A successful prosecution needs the methodical collection of evidence and cannot be rushed. Once we have made an arrest we have very limited amount of time to question the suspects and bring charges. I have no intention of standing in front of a Magistrate with insufficient evidence and, as a result, having my case thrown out.' He looked down his long nose at Wright with disdain. 'Also I have no idea who this Mr Sniper is.'

Peter Wright tried hard to contain his temper. He recognized Smith's type, overweight and with little imagination and too much self-importance. He sat behind his desk belittling the six-month's work of the security services obviously out of his depth with this case. He bit back his sarcasm determined to manage the man. 'Detective Superintendent, together we have the opportunity to crack one of the most serious spy rings to have betrayed Britain since Burgess and McLean. If you have any doubts about the strength of the evidence against Lonsdale in particular, I suggest you join me tonight in the flat where we can monitor Lonsdale's communications with Moscow.'

So on the evening of January 6th George Smith joined Wright in a flat adjoining Lonsdale's. There were already two technicians in residence with their heads clamped in earphones. The room smelled of stale fish and chips. Wright did not bother to introduce the others who didn't even look up. 'They are listening into microphones we have placed in Lonsdale's flat,' Wright explained. 'There's one in the bathroom, one in the bedroom and third in the lounge incorporated into his telephone. Lonsdale is currently at a club in Soho but usually gets home shortly before midnight almost always with a companion.'

Smith wanted to ask to see the magistrate's warrant to authorise this snooping, but suspected that there wasn't one. He wisely decided not to pursue that matter. 'If the KGB already know of *Sniper's* defection they will warn Lonsdale on the 3.00 a.m. radio transmission,' Wright advised. 'If that happens you should arrest him immediately or he'll be gone. Smith did not like being told what to do by a civilian, but he couldn't find fault with this suggestion so he just grunted a response.

Around midnight Gordon Lonsdale returned to his flat with a young lady. The sound quality of the listening devices was excellent and during a particularly amorous session an embarrassed Smith ordered the technician to turn the volume down. Possibly because of Lonsdale's lengthy sexual encounter he did not turn to his short wave radio at three o'clock and by 3.30 both occupants of the flat appeared to be sleeping. The female was woken by Lonsdale at 7.00 and left the flat almost immediately. Lonsdale went to the bathroom to shave, where the second microphone picked him up, whistling what one of the MI5 officers told Smith was a Russian folk song. 'That is not in itself evidence of espionage,' the policeman pronounced. He did however agree to make the arrests that day.

Weymouth police phoned through to say that Houghton and Gee had left by train for their monthly rendezvous with Lonsdale. Smith's plan was simple. Lonsdale would be followed from his flat by one team and a second would follow Houghton and Gee from Waterloo. When they met they would be arrested. He said nothing could go wrong and surprisingly it didn't. Smith himself was present on Waterloo Bridge in an unmarked police car and saw the three meet. Lonsdale was carrying a brown paper parcel, which he handed to Houghton. Gee had a paper carrier bag, which she thrust into Lonsdale's hand as a marked police car drew to a halt next to them. All three were handcuffed and as senior officer present George Smith advised each of them that they were under arrest on suspicion of espionage. A third police car arrived on the scene and each of the suspects was put in the back of a different car and taken to Special Branch Headquarters which Smith reckoned would be more secure than Scotland Yard. He knew it was important that they did not have an opportunity to fabricate a story together and didn't want news of the arrests to leak to the papers before he had secured the rest of the gang. Besides, he had his own friends in the press pack, who would give him a good write up in return for an exclusive

Because arrest was no surprise to Lonsdale he was able to enjoy himself in the interview room. His instructions from Moscow were quite clear; give away as little as possible. He recognized Smith as a vainglorious and rather stupid man and determined to make his life as difficult as possible. He refused to confirm his name or address smiling a superior sort of smile. Inspector Smith blustered, threatened and cajoled and Lonsdale said nothing. When he offered the Inspector a tit-bit, it was always something already known. The increasingly frustrated policeman was led up blind alleys and dead ends. When Lonsdale was told that an immediate confession would help his case he asked for that to be put in writing. Two hours of fruitless interrogation left Smith fuming. As he wanted to be present when Peter and Helen Kroger were arrested he decided to put a stop to the farce and abruptly left. One of his officers was instructed to remove Lonsdale's tie, shoelaces and belt to ensure he did not have the means to commit suicide.

At five o'clock that evening Peter Wright received a message, 'Superintendent Smith has asked me to let you know that *Last Act* is finished.' He knew Lonsdale had been arrested, but guessed that many questions were still unanswered.

Chapter 17
Tidying Up

'This is Detective Superintendent George Smith of Special Branch. May I speak to Mr Peter Wright?'

Wright seized the telephone from the switchboard operator. 'Wright here.'

'I have them both in the bag Mr Wright. I shall be bringing them to HQ straight away. Two constables are even now collecting evidence, of which there seems to be a great deal.'

'Tell them to hold everything till I arrive with a scene of crime team,' Wright yelled down the phone. 'They're not to touch anything. They have no idea what they are looking for.'

'There's no need to shout Mr Wright. They are both very experienced police officers.'

'Please ask them to wait for me.' Peter Wright tried to contain his temper and mollify the outraged dignity of Superintendent Smith. 'Also if you can delay making any announcement for 48 hours we have a chance of catching Moscow on the hop.' He drove as fast as he could to Ruislip swearing at the rush-hour traffic, which seemed determined to thwart him. When he arrived at 45 Cranley Drive he found two young PCs systematically ripping the downstairs sitting room apart.

He waved his identity card in their faces. 'Stop what you're doing at once,' he shouted almost weeping with rage and frustration. 'Haven't you any regard for even basic preservation of evidence.'

'Inspector Smith has told us to prioritise the securing of forensic evidence.' The older of the two constables attempted to preserve his dignity in the face of this outburst.

Wright tried to control himself and to speak a little more calmly. 'Surely you've heard of the need for an unbroken chain of custody? If you've collected evidence ignoring this, any self-respecting court may rule it inadmissible. This case however will not be going to any tupenny-halfpenny magistrates court but without doubt to the Old Bailey itself.' He felt sick at the thought of Lord Parker sarcastically ruling against everything they had found. *God knows how much that might have been useful they had already destroyed with their ham-fisted approach*, he thought. 'I've called for a professional scene of crime team from the Security Service. You can either stay and learn something useful, or push off now.' The officer who had spoken up took fright at Wright's show of temper and left a little sheepishly. The younger constable, a WPC, seemed a little more intelligent than her colleague and decided to stay. 'Keep quiet and watch,' Wight ordered. The two sat in an uncomfortable silence while waiting for the Crime Scene Examiners to arrived. 'What's your name,' Peter eventually asked her.'

'WPC Streeter, Sir.' She said in little more than a whisper.

'No I mean your Christian name; the name that defines you as a person.'

'Samantha, Sir, but my family and colleagues usually call me Sam.'

'Well Sam, my name is Peter.' He paused to let the informality sink in. 'Tell me about the arrest.'

'Three of us from Scotland Yard were ordered to come here and wait in the next street for someone from Special Branch to give us further orders.' Sam looked down at her feet trying to straighten the facts in her head. 'Around 5.00 pm the Super and another officer, both in plain clothes rolled up. He told us he had an arrest warrant but needed to gain an entry to No 45 first. He would pretend to be looking into a complaint by neighbours. PC Dawkins and me, he's the one who's just left, we were told to go round the back and make sure no one escaped. By the time we got inside the Super was reading them their rights. She, that is Mrs Kroger, looked like a nice old lady. (Anyone over 45 probably looked old to this youngster). She was in a bit of a tizz and kept saying 'Oh dear, what is this all about?' and stuff like that. Mr Kroger was saying nothing, just looking stunned.'

Sam paused to see if her story was going down all right. Peter nodded for her to continue. 'Before the Super took them off Mrs K asked if she could check on the Aga in the kitchen as it was playing up a bit. I was told to escort her. I noticed she had taken some papers from her handbag and was just in time to stop her pushing them into the fire. I guessed it could be evidence she wanted to destroy though she still looked pretty innocent. I've got the bag here.' She picked up a brown leather handbag that was lying on the sofa.

Peter opened it carefully. In a zipped compartment he found some code pads and signal plan for high-speed transmissions; the sort Moscow used. This was the jackpot he had hoped for. 'Has the handbag had been under your control at all times?'

He stared at her hard so that she could have no doubt that this was not a causal question.

Sam nodded 'yes' with hardly a hesitation. That was good enough. He could claim the chain of evidence had been preserved. 'You did well,' Peter told and she blushed very prettily. The team from MI5 arrived shortly after this and started a systematic and professional search. They quickly found a bottle of magnetic iron oxide used to print out Morse from the high-speed messages onto tape without being transferred onto a sophisticated recorder and slowed down. In a hidden compartment in the chest of drawers in the bedroom they found false passports, money and microdots which eventually when magnified turned out to be personal letters to Lonsdale's wife. It took some time but eventually they uncovered sufficient evidence to convict both Paul and Helen Kroger for conspiracy to commit espionage, though it was nine days with the most thorough of searches before they eventually located the transmitter hidden in a cavity under the kitchen floor.

Chapter 19
Check Mate

'Only my friends call me Bunty. To everyone else I am either Ethel or Miss Gee. You may call me Miss Gee.' Ethel sat on a hard metal chair opposite Superintendent Smith, upright in a grey denim prison suit but composed. If he had expected her to crumble and dissolve he was disappointed. Throughout her interrogation she had stuck rigidly to her story. She believed Commander Alex Johnson was in the US Navy and had been helping him test the level of security at Portland.

'On Waterloo Bridge you handed a package to Lonsdale, the man you call Johnson. I saw you and will say so at your trial. This package contained not only the blueprints of HMS Dreadnought, but also three other files clearly marked Top Secret. You must have known this was wrong.'

'If as you tell me the man I know as Commander Johnson is not in the American Navy, then I have made a terrible mistake. I will confess to that mistake, but I was unaware that I was helping a spy.' She thought back to the happy times she and Harry had spent with Alex. *Has it all been deceit*? She asked herself. Superintendent Smith was increasingly frustrated with her.

Interviewing Houghton had been comparatively easy. Once Harry had been cautioned he began to babble out a sort of confession trying to turn Queen's Evidence. He listed a string of contacts with names like Nikki, George and Roman and swore that he would be happy to speak against any of them.

This didn't sound promising to the Superintendent. He suspected that some of those named would have diplomatic immunity, and any Silk would tear strips off Houghton's evidence in court. Sifting the truth from the exaggeration and lies would take time, but the Superintendent already had sufficient forensic evidence to guarantee his conviction. A search of Harry's cottage near Weymouth had produced a wireless transmitter in his living room which he found difficult to explain away, a cigarette lighter with false bottom similar to the one found in Lonsdale's flat, and a coffee flask with a secret container. In addition the searchers had found a tin buried in the garden stacked with money. The boffins were still counting it, but there appeared to be more than £9,000. This Houghton claimed, were his savings from Warsaw, but a simple check on serial numbers had disproved that. The one consistency in his story was he was adamant that Ethel knew nothing of spying.

Back with Ethel Gee Smith tried a different tack. 'Is Houghton your lover?'

'That's my business not yours,' Ethel retorted.

'I'll take that as a 'yes' then,' Smith said.

'You can take it how you like,' Ethel snapped back. 'My answer is the same.'

'Your precious lover has owned up to everything.' He picked up a paper that had been lying on the desk between them and started to read from it. 'He has told us exactly what the two of you were up to and that you were fully aware that Lonsdale was passing all your documents to the Russians. He said the charade about Alex Johnson working for the American Navy was only for the first meeting, and that you have been fully aware of the truth for months. We found £4,747 hidden in your bedroom. How did a filing clerk on £10 a week manage to save that? Houghton told us that Lonsdale regularly handed over considerable sums of money to both of you. How do you account for that?'

Though Ethel had already accepted she would have to take responsibility for her actions, she knew with absolute certainty that Harry would not have implicated her more than was absolutely necessary even to protect himself. 'The money is my savings from a variety of sources and I am not changing my story as it's the truth.'

Superintendent Smith continued to be bad tempered and feel thwarted. Despite Peter Wright's request for a 48-hour news blackout he had enjoyed conducting a highly successful news conference with selected journalists the day after the arrest of all five members of the Portland Spy Ring. He had sold the story as a triumph for British policing omitting any mention of the contribution of the security services. Now the date of the trial at The Old Bailey was fixed for the second week in March he had to complete his interrogation of the accused and charge them. He was personally convinced of the guilt of all of them, but could a jury be persuaded they were guilty beyond reasonable doubt?

Despite all the evidence collected from their Ruislip House Peter and Helen Kroger denied any knowledge of espionage. The Superintendent had tried interviewing husband and wife separately. Helen maintained the charade of middle-aged housewife who knew nothing of what had been going on and had been badly let down by Gordon Lonsdale who she thought was a friend. She could not explain the false passports. Peter Kroger insisted that he was nothing more than a book dealer whose interests went no further than playing cricket for the local team. He then clammed up complaining of faintness. In the hope of obtaining further evidence the police allowed the Krogers to share a room which was heavily bugged, but their conversation was nothing more than you might expect from a suburban couple who claimed to be wrongfully arrested.

Smith, though he admitted it to no one, had a sneaking admiration for Lonsdale. The spy was not putting up any sort of defence, made no excuses and accepted responsibility for all the equipment found in his friends' house claiming they knew nothing about it. Unlike the other four, Smith accepted that he alone had not betrayed his country. As there was no direct evidence that either Peter or Helen Kroger had actually sent information to Russia the lawyers had persuaded him to amend the charges against them to that of conspiracy to commit espionage rather than spying itself. Lonsdale's conviction was a certainty, but with his silent mocking, this knowledge gave surprisingly little satisfaction.

Houghton's confession was sufficient to guarantee a guilty verdict, but would Ethel Gee's flimsy excuses sway a jury?

**

The trial, which was conducted in camera by Lord Chief Justice Parker, began on 13th March 1961. Either evidence was too secret to allow the public and press to be present, or the establishment was too embarrassed to reveal the scale of the conspiracy. The combined efforts of British Intelligence, the CIA and the Canadian Mounties were unable to uncover the true identity of Lonsdale, so it was under the name Gordon Henry Lonsdale that he was tried. He refused to speak in his own defence merely making a statement at the end claiming that the Krogers knew nothing. Moscow must have been delighted. Houghton and Gee sat together in the dock looking nervously around the courtroom throughout the trial. Harry gave rambling often-incoherent answers to the prosecution questions while Ethel stuck to the story she had told Superintendent Smith. The Krogers pleaded confused innocence throughout. They too refused to take the stand. The trial lasted seven days.

Smith need not have worried. The British public had had enough of being made fools of by the KGB. Spy after spy had escaped punishment and now the jury had a chance to represent public opinion. They deliberated for 80 minutes and all defendants were found guilty of all charges.

The Lord Chief Justice also was in no mood to show leniency. After congratulating the jury on their swift and accurate verdict he addressed each of the accused in turn.

'Houghton, your defence that you were subject to threats and beatings by both Polish and Russian agents and your actions were motivated by a desire to protect your ex-wife and Miss Gee from violence is not supported by the evidence produced by the prosecution. For many years you have engaged in espionage activities with scant regard for the consequences. It is now time for you to face those consequences and I sentence you to 15 years in custody.

Miss Gee, you claim that you only knew Gordon Lonsdale as Alex Johnson, a Commander in the American Navy and that in all your actions you were misled and motivated by love for Houghton. This excuse suggests a level of naivety or stupidity quite at odds to the other evidence of you character that the court has heard. Your defence is a tissue of lies and the fact is you were motivated by greed and the possibility of making easy money. Like Houghton I sentence you to 15 years in custody.

Peter and Helen Kroger, you have both been found guilty of being involved in a complex and sophisticate espionage ring. Despite your claims to be innocent bystanders caught up in the machination of others, your refusal to take the stand to explain your actions and the wealth of complicit espionage material found at your house in Ruislip in particular the false Canadian passports gave the lie to your claim merely to be a second hand bookseller and suburban housewife. I am confident that you were at the centre of a major espionage effort against the United Kingdom. This opinion is supported by Inspector Smith producing proof to the court after the jury found guilty that your real names are Morris and Lona Cohen, wanted in America by the FBI on earlier charges of espionage and I sentence each of you to 20 years in custody

Lonsdale, like your friends Mr and Mrs Kroger you have refused to speak to the court in your own defence. Your counsel has pleaded for you that at least it can be said that you were not a traitor to your country. This is true however not sufficient mitigation to prevent the severest of prison sentences as you were the directing force of a spy ring that has struck at the heart of the security of this country. I sentence you to 25 years in custody.

Officers, take them down.'

Postscript

After only three years in jail Gordon Lonsdale was exchanged for the British spy Greville Wynne who had been imprisoned in Lubyanka Prison since 1963. Lonsdale, or Konon Molody to give him back his correct name, returned to Moscow a hero. Despite this the Russians gave him positions of surprisingly minor importance and according to George Blake who met him in Moscow he became critical of the Soviet authorities and took to drink. He died on a mushroom picking expedition in 1970 aged 48.

In 1969 the Krogers were exchanged for the British student, Gerald Brooke, who had been imprisoned in Russia for importing anti-Soviet literature. As part of the deal the Russians admitted the pair had been spies. Back in Moscow, as Morris and Lona Cohen, they were awarded the Order of the Red Banner. Morris continued to train Russian agents up to his death in 1995. Lona died in 1992.

Harry Houghton and Ethel Gee served nine years of their sentence before being released. They were married in 1971 and lived in Dorset until their deaths

Sir Roger Hollis was Director of MI5 from 1956 to 1965. In 1964 the FLUENCY committee was established whose sole purpose was to uncover any serious penetration by the KGB and the GRU of the British security services. In his book *Spycatcher*, Peter Wright, who chaired FLUENCY from1964-1970, claimed conclusive evidence that during this period the Soviet authorities had a high level penetration of MI5. The soviet defector Igor Gouzenko identified a high-level mole in the organisation code name *Elli*. After exhaustive enquiries by the FLUENCY Committee suspicion fell on Roger Hollis. In 1969 his loyalty was subjected to a full investigation and interrogation, but the results were inconclusive. He died in 1973 still under suspicion and is buried in an unmarked grave. His son Adrian became a chess Grandmaster.

Peter Wright remained convinced that the reason Lonsdale/Molody returned from Moscow in late 1960 despite the Russians being aware that his cover was blown, was to protect an even more important spy at the very top of MI5. Before Molody died in suspicious circumstances aged 48, he began to blame the Russian authorities for not withdrawing him from England in 1960 when they had the chance before his arrest.

Could the Director of MI5 have been a Soviet agent?

Historical Note

All conversations in this story are fiction. This is a work of fiction as facts are in short supply. Hopefully I have managed to write what is somewhere near the truth. Both Harry Houghton and Konon Molody wrote autobiographies. Houghton's is called *Operation Portland: Autobiography of a Spy*. Molody's, published in 1965 is called *Spy*. Both books are so full of lies as to be unreliable as evidence and were the reason for my title *All Lies*.

Spy Catcher by Peter Wright was published in 1987 and was banned from sale in Britain by the Thatcher Government. This book and *Their Trade is Treachery* by Chapman Pincher both throw doubt on the loyalty of Sir Roger Hollis.

The true story of *Buster Crabb: the Headless Frogman* has never been made public by the British Government, nor have any details about the extent of the espionage of Houghton and Gee.